WITHDRAWN

checkers

checkers

john marsden

Houghton Mifflin Company
Boston 1998

Acknowledgments

Many thanks to Kylee Ervine, Ros Alexander and Bronwyn Miller.

The characters and events in this book are fictitious, and any resemblance to actual persons or events is purely coincidental.

First published in 1996 by Pan Macmillan Australia Pty Limited, Sydney

The text of this book is set in eleven point Utopia.

Library of Congress Cataloging-in-Publication Data

Marsden, John, 1950–
Checkers / John Marsden.
p. cm.
Summary: Speaking from a mental hospital, a teenage girl recounts the tremendous media pressure that preceded the breaking scandal of her father's unethical business dealings.
ISBN 0-395-85754-6
[1. Psychiatric hospitals—Fiction. 2. Mental illness—Fiction. 3. Dogs—Fiction. 4. Family problems—Fiction. 5. Australia—Fiction.] I. Title.
PZ7.M35145Ch 1998
[Fic] 97-49405 CIP AC

To Albie,
who jumped fences,
chased rabbits,
and barked at life

an aussie glossary

aggro aggressive

BM BMW

boardies surfing shorts

botting to get by begging, mooching

chooks chickens

corked twisted

crack on to to try to date someone

D&Ms humorous word for 'deep and meaningful' conversations

drafts the game of checkers

dump snowfall

durry cigarette

flat apartment

give the flick to get rid of someone

goss gossip

interstate in another state

jumper sweater

kiosk a small shop

linen press linen closet

Merc Mercedes

op-shop store that sells second-hand clothes for charity

pokey small and dark

prawnhead nerd

roundabout rotary

rusk sticks hard breadsticks for babies to chew on

scabbing borrowing with little intention of paying back

shadow minister a politician from an opposition party who monitors the politician in the government party who is responsible for a specific area

shelf company a company that is created with little money or function in order to be used by a big business

sooling inciting

UDL brand name for a line of alcoholic drinks

wanker someone who is conceited, insensitive, and self-indulgent

wanky being conceited, insensitive, self-indulgent

wonky not functioning properly

one

IT'S SO QUIET. I don't know what the time is, maybe two o'clock, three o'clock. I think I've been asleep for a couple of hours; I'm not sure.

Sister Llosa's on tonight, with Hanna. Sister Llosa's a big suntanned yak, and Hanna's a shining white lizard who slips in and out of the rooms quickly and quietly. Most nights when they're on together they murmur away at the desk. It's like a lullaby. I don't hear the words but I hear their soft voices playing music with each other, Sister Llosa deep and dark, Hanna light and laughing.

Right now they're not at the desk, though. They might be in 109 with the new admission. He was yelling for hours when he first came in, but he's quiet now, too. Everything's quiet suddenly. There's no snoring, no hiss and grind from the lift, none of the bathroom promenades: the shuffle-shuffle-creak-piddle-flush-creak shuffle-shuffle. That's the sound I hate most. I'd rather have screaming than that.

I'm glad I've got my own room now. I've always had my own bedroom, for as long as I remember. School camps are the only times I ever slept with anyone else.

"Shared the room" with anyone else, I mean. God, I hate how everything you say sounds like it has to do with sex. I do hate that.

Last year at school we were talking about Daniel Morrissey and I said "Daniel sucks," and Tanya said "Yeah, you'd know."

That's the kind of thing I mean.

It was the way everyone laughed at me, that's what I'm really talking about. You get scared to say anything, through fear of the laughing. Laughter's meant to be loving, wrapping itself around you like a hug, but when it's aimed at me it seems cruel.

I was better off than some people, though. Simone, I don't know how she stood it, being put down all the time, by everyone, even teachers. Trying to make a joke and listening to us, the cruel mockingbirds, as we told her what we thought of her joke. Trying to find a partner in Drama, waiting to be asked and finally having to be put with someone by Ms Eddy, while the other person rolled her eyes and stood as far away as possible. Sitting on her own up the front of the bus when we went on excursions. I shivered when I watched Simone. I knew that could so easily be me. What makes some people unpopular? Simone does everything right. She lives in Ralston Avenue, in a huge house with two Mercs parked in the drive; she goes to Mt Silver in winter and Providence Bay in summer; her father runs Conway

Carpets and a heap of other companies. They won the Oaks four years ago with Admiral Sam.

I mean, what else do you have to do? How many points does it take? How many points do you need?

That's why I'd shivered when I'd looked at Simone. I'd counted my own points enough times. For years I'd looked at my friends and wondered. Sally, Zoe, Jana, Shon. Kym, before she moved back to America. What was it that they liked in me? If I'd made a mistake, would that have been it? If I'd had a different name, a different family, if I'd lived in Lennon or Everett West and wore clothes from Reward, would I have stopped being their friend and instead become a guest on *Oprah?* "Teen with No Friends". . . "The Teen Everyone Hates". . . "From Teen Queen to Freak Queen."

Life seems so fragile. You walk down the centre of the highway, with the big trucks rushing past. They make the air shake. They blow you off your line. You stick out your arms to get your balance. A truck hits one arm and spins you around. You stagger and fall, holding your arm and crying. Another truck rushes at you. There's no escape. Your body's just bones and flesh, that's all. There are too many things beating at you, blowing at you, hurting you and leaving bruises.

It's a miracle anyone survives to be a teenager. It's a miracle any teenager survives to be an adult.

There is noise out in the corridor again now. Lots of footsteps, people being busy, hushed voices. I can see shadows going backwards and forwards, passing quickly under the door. You can tell the staff footsteps from the patients'. The staff sound like they're going somewhere.

I imagine they're admitting another new patient. You get them in the middle of the night sometimes. That's when Esther came in, and Emine.

I wish I could sleep. I want to sleep; but the more I want to, the less I can. I never used to have problems with sleeping. So many new things have happened lately: this is just one more. It makes me wonder who's now inhabiting my body: what is this confusion of feelings and thoughts that I keep inside. It's not only the things outside that threaten my balance. The feelings storm through me, up and down and all around, crashing into each other and falling back, reeling and rubbing their noses. I contain them all but I often wonder what would happen if they broke out. The Luna Park of my mind would spill onto the streets. Whole cities would be overrun. Crazy desperate figures would chase each other across the landscape. It's important that I keep them inside, but it's all I can do to hold them there. They want to erupt. I'm saving the world by stopping them.

In the Dayroom yesterday Daniel said to me, "Maybe something good will come out of our being here."

"What?" I said.

He thought for a long time then said, "Maybe we'll learn more about ourselves. Find parts of ourselves we never knew we had."

"But I don't want to find any new parts," I whined. "I was happy the way I was."

I wasn't, of course. But I hardly knew it: that's the difference. Anyway, it's one of the games we play in here, pretending we were huge social successes in our past lives. Esther's about the only one who doesn't play that game, and Emine sometimes.

The noises in the corridor are getting quieter, duller. It seems darker now, and colder. I feel that I know every minute of the days and nights in here. I like that, in some ways. There have been times here, many of them, when all I've wanted was to get out, go home; other times when I want to stay in here forever. At this moment I want to stay forever. I feel safe here. They know me. I don't think they'll hurt me. I like the little things, the safe little things that never change: the queue at the nurses' station for medication, the games of table tennis in the Dayroom, the changes of shifts, even the corny way Dr Singh comes in each morning and says, "And how is Miss Warner today?"

I think he likes having me as his patient. Whenever either of us mentions my father, Dr Singh swells a little and looks important. I'm used to that, so I notice it easily.

Another reason I don't want to leave at the moment is the painting on the wall in this room. It's dumb to like it, because it looks nothing like Checkers. But I pretend it does and I lie here liking it. The dog in the painting is about half the size of Checkers and reddish brown instead of black and white, and he's lying on a rug in front of a fire, which Checkers never did, because although we had a fireplace we never had a fire.

In this dark room, if I look at the painting and look away quickly, I can make it seem like it might be Checkers.

Getting Checkers was one of the two perfect nights of my life. The other was my twelfth birthday, when it just so happened that everything went like a dream and everyone left saying it was the best party they'd ever been to. There have only been two perfect nights, but I don't complain about that. If I have a complaint it's that both nights lied to me: the perfection was pretence. But sometimes I think it was still worth it, almost. On those two nights I thought that life itself was going to be perfect.

Dad came home with Checkers, but with no warning. It had been such a normal evening. I was in my room doing homework. To be exact, I was halfway through a project on AIDS. Mark was watching *Captain Comet:* I'd deliberately left my bedroom door open so I could hear. Mum was in the kitchen. I don't know what she was doing but I can guess. Cleaning. We had the whitest kitchen in the Southern Hemisphere but she wasn't risking having anyone take her title away. We had a cleaning lady come in but it was never enough. Mum polished tiles till it looked like they were painted.

I'd argued and pestered and plagued everyone for a dog. Mark wanted one too, but not in the way I did. He wanted a dog because I wanted one, because all his friends had one, because that's what kids have. He's so materialistic that it scares me, and revolts me. He didn't think of dogs as dogs, just as more objects to collect.

Anyway, I heard Dad drive in, much earlier than usual. And he stopped in the driveway too. That was odd. I glanced through the window. He was already out of the driver's seat and doing a funny kind of John Cleese walk to the door, long strides that were getting him to the house in a hurry. He looked very intent, very concentrated. I thought he'd forgotten something, that he was calling in on the way to a meeting to pick up some notes or grab a clean shirt or give Mum a message. I turned back to my project and wrote "with their friends or family, or in a hospice," then I became aware of the yabber of excited voices from the kitchen. I went out and there they all were: Dad beaming and hugging Mum and talking flat out, Mum smiling and looking pleased and letting herself be hugged, and Mark hugging himself, going, "Bonus, bonus, we'll be so rich."

"What's the party?" I asked.

"We can have anything we want for our birthdays," Mark said, all in one breath, really fast, like he couldn't believe it and wanted to scream.

"Within reason," Mum said quickly.

I started to realise what must have happened.

"You got the contract," I said to Dad.

He nodded hard, with his lips pressed tight together.

"But you're not allowed to tell anyone," Mark said.

I started to feel excited too. Like, I don't think I'm materialistic, and I hate the way Mark is, but I'm not Mother Teresa either. The possibilities were opening in my mind like flowers and I thought, "Jeez, this could be huge." They were all watching me, waiting for my reaction, and I said, "Wow, God, fantastic, Dad. You did it!"

"Oh well, with a little help from my friends," he said modestly.

But I felt they were somehow disappointed with me, that I hadn't quite been able to show enough excitement. Not spontaneous enough. So I kept going, but I think I went on too long then. "That's great, Dad, fantastic. You legend. You actually did it. Jack must be so rapt."

He let go of Mum and went to the fridge. "It'll make a big difference to us," he said. "It'll be the end of our financial problems. I'll be able to get you all the things I've always wanted, all the things I've dreamed of us having."

"Can we really have whatever we want for our birthdays?" I asked.

But Dad had paused, ice tongs in one hand, glass in the other. "Oh!" he cried. "How could I forget?"

He dropped everything on the bench and rushed outside. We all stared out the window to see what he was doing. He was already back at the car, opening the rear door. As we watched he pulled out a large cardboard box, about the size of Mark's old stereo speaker. He carried it triumphantly but awkwardly up the path and through the door, as we crowded around, curious to see what our new life was already bringing.

"Lucky I didn't leave him there," Dad said. He put the box on the table. "Poor thing wouldn't have been too happy."

I heard a soft rustling from the box and realised it was something alive. I knew at once what it must be. I untied the string carefully, trying to stop Mark from getting under my elbow, and I opened the box.

And there he was.

Checkers.

two

IT'S BEEN SO BORING here the last few days. In Group we seem to be going round in circles. I'm sick of Cindy talking about her parents' divorce. Sometimes I think the only reason Cindy really cares is that her father sold their Mt Simpson flat as part of the settlement. Cindy's weekend skiing trips melted like September snow.

But Cindy gives her little talk every day and sits there sobbing, then Emine gives her a hug, and Marj says sympathetic therapist-type things like, "It's a very sad feeling, the feeling of being abandoned," and I roll my eyes and wonder what's on *Oprah.*

Marj's big new thing is tree planting. She figures it's good for us to do "positive life-affirming things," so the last three afternoons, since I wrote that other stuff in this old notebook in the middle of the night, we've all headed off to plant trees in the hospital grounds. There's nothing wrong with it, I suppose; I mean, I'm all in favour of planting trees—who isn't?—but we don't actually get a lot done. Marj plants four to every one we put in. Oliver and I sit against the fence and smoke and talk about ourselves and play with the fallen leaves and watch Marj working. Esther walks around in a figure-of-eight pattern, humming. I think she really might be quite crazy. Emine does a bit of digging. Cindy listens to her Walkman, which seriously irritates Marj. Ben—nervous, restless, irritating Ben, his dark face always watching you to guess what you're thinking—goes from person to person looking for someone he can talk to for more than thirty seconds before they give him the flick. In Group he complains that no-one likes him, and that's true, but no-one dislikes him either. You just wish he'd stand still and talk normally and honestly for once, instead of his: "Hey, look at this bit of bark, you know what it reminds me of, huh, are you having any visitors tomorrow, my mum might come, wonder what Esther's doing now, she's going to wear a path around that tree, hey do you want to watch that video again tonight, Emine does, I think I'll take a survey, like get everyone to vote, well might go and see if Marj wants a hand, see you . . ."

Daniel hangs around us a lot, trying not to get his hands dirty, but also trying to crack on to Oliver. He's obsessed with Oliver. Oliver doesn't mind him, he's gentle with him, but then Oliver's a gentle guy, gentle with everyone, maybe that's his problem. I like Daniel, and I'm sort of fascinated by him. I've never met anyone so openly gay, and it seems amazing at his age, at our age. He's comfortable with me, with all the girls really.

I suppose he doesn't feel threatened by us. For that matter I suppose we don't feel threatened by him. He's more like a girl in some ways: the more girly we are, the more he likes it. He gets so excited about our clothes and make-up and stuff. I'm a big disappointment to him because I'm not very girly: I'd rather play basketball than talk about my hair. We sort of tease Daniel a bit, and we probably shouldn't, but I can't help it and I don't think he minds. He's only got us really. Oliver's nice to him but they don't go off and have big D & Ms or anything. Ben's so nervous of him that when Daniel comes within a hundred metres it's like Ben needs an instant Largactil shot, 200 mls, stat.

Anyway, it was Checkers I set out to write about, but I keep getting distracted. I was remembering that first day, the feeling of opening the box, hoping it might be a dog but still scared to hope too much in case I was disappointed. I wasn't disappointed. There was a pair of bright eyes, an outsize head cocked to one side, a pink tongue, a grinning cheeky mouth, and an outrageous white and black body that looked like the tiles on our bathroom floor might if there was an earthquake. His coat was like crazy paving. I fell totally in love with him, straightaway. He had such an alert head on such a crazy wacky body. He was so unlike the Jack Russells and golden retrievers and standard poodles that everyone's got around our neighbourhood.

And he was so different to the kind of dog that I'd have expected Dad to get. With Dad, it was like everything had to be the way everyone else did it. Our house was exactly like you'd expect the Finance Director of Rider Group to live in. We had the two BMs, because that's what you have if you live the way we did. We got the house at Providence Bay because that's where everyone goes, and whenever we were there Dad wore La Mer or P&S or Heritage: shirts, shorts, jeans, boardies, didn't matter, whatever it was it'd be one of those labels. It was so exciting for Mark and me every morning at breakfast, trying to guess which label he'd have on today. Sometimes I wished he'd go and get something from an op-shop or Dimmey's—anything to prove that he didn't do things just because our friends did, or because someone powerful, like Jack, told him to.

Yes, one of the few times in his life that I've known Dad to do something unpredictable and different was the night he came home with Checkers.

I picked Checkers up and held him against me. He wasn't the kind of dog you hug really tight, like a Labrador. Right away I sensed that. He had too much independence, too much pride. He gave my nose a long lick, which freaked Mum right out, then he took an eager look around. It was like he was saying, "Right, which way's the great outdoors? I've got a lot of exploring to do." I put him down. Mum said, "Oh, not on the floor. Murray, I don't want him in the house." Checkers immediately spread his back legs and did a little piss. I gave him a smack on the nose and airfreighted him outside, leaving Mum to clean up the puddle. Checkers didn't seem at all discombobulated (I love that word) by the smack on the nose. He zigzagged around the yard like James at the Year 10 formal. I could hear Mum trying to start an argument about the dog but Dad was still too high to get into that: he wouldn't listen.

Mark came outside with me and Checkers. "What are you going to get for your birthday?" he wanted to know.

"I don't know." I was cross with him for even thinking about that when something so exciting as a dog had arrived in our lives.

"I want a motorbike," he said.

"Well, good for you." Then I added: "What's the use of a motorbike? There's nowhere to ride it round here."

"I don't care, I'll find a place. I just want one."

"What do you reckon we should call the dog?"

I was asking him but I already felt the dog was mine. I'd felt that from the moment Dad carried the box into the house—and it was sort of understood and accepted by everyone else too, without anything actually being said. I suppose it was because I was the one who'd been begging for so long.

Mark just glanced at him and said, "He's the dumbest-looking dog I've ever seen. What did Dad have to get one like that for? I wanted a red setter, like the Wakefields and the Stewarts."

"Honestly, Mark, why do you always have to be the same as everyone else?"

"Why do you always have to be different to everyone else?"

"I'm not."

"Well, I'm not the same as everyone else. I just like red setters, that's all. Is that a crime?"

"Well, anyway, what are we going to call him?"

"I don't know. He looks like the bathroom floor, doesn't he? He looks like someone smashed all the tiles up in the bathroom. Call him Bathroom Floor."

"He looks like a chessboard."

"OK, call him that then."

"Chessboard? That's the name of the Walkleys' horse that won all those races. The Rawson Stakes. I'm not calling him that. They'll think we got it off them."

"Call him Drafts then. Or Checkers."

"Checkers? That's not bad. I quite like that."

When we told Dad later that we'd chosen "Checkers" he looked quite shocked.

"Is that a joke?" he wanted to know.

We didn't understand what he was talking about.

"No. How do you mean? He just looks like a chessboard, that's all, but we didn't want to call him that because of the Walkleys' horse. So we thought we'd call him Checkers instead."

He calmed down then and even seemed amused.

"I suppose it is quite appropriate," he muttered, and went back to reading *BRW.*

We went to dinner that night to celebrate the contract. We met at Jack and Rosie's. They were all there: Bruce and Mona, Doug and Emma, Dermot and Chris, and all the various kids. Everyone was just as high as Dad. Jack was off his head, mad, drunk with the knowledge of all the money he was going to make. While I was watching him I reckon he drank half a bottle of Scotch, but it didn't have the slightest effect. He was getting off all right, but not on alcohol. He could have drunk tomato juice and he wouldn't have come down one bit.

The party did get wilder and noisier, though. Half an hour after we got there Jack had a pair of scissors and was chasing all the men around. Every time he grabbed one he cut his tie off, about a centimetre from the knot. The cheapest tie would have been a hundred and fifty bucks, but they all thought it was the best joke of the year.

The idea was that we'd go to a restaurant, but Dermot talked Jack out of it because no-one was meant to know that they'd got the contract. As Dermot said, if we all arrived in a restaurant yelling and laughing and celebrating, it'd be on the front page of tomorrow's papers. Drunk or sober, Jack was smart enough to understand that. He suddenly turned on us kids and gave us a long talk about how we mustn't tell anyone or it'd be bigger than the collapse of the Weimar Republic. I hated Jack when he talked to us like that and I hated the parents, the way they stood there and let him do it. We all knew Jack controlled our lives, but I didn't like being reminded of it.

I was pleased we weren't eating out, though, because I had Checkers with me and I'd been worried about how I was going to smuggle him into a restaurant. Jack called a pizza place and, without asking anyone what they wanted, ordered twice as many pizzas as we could eat. "Good news for Checkers," I thought. We kids went down to the poolroom and shot pool and watched TV and boasted to each other about how cool we were.

I got sick of it pretty soon and played with Checkers. I didn't like any of them much, and the conversation was so hyped up and wanky that it made me sick. Eventually I fell asleep in a corner of the room with Checkers sucking on my finger. The yelling and laughing of the adults from one end of the house was echoing the screaming of the kids as they wrestled and told pathetic jokes and chucked pizza at each other.

I read this back and I think it sounds terrible: I sound terrible, like a square. I don't feel like a square but perhaps I am. Here in the hospital it doesn't matter so much. Because there's not many of us, us teenagers I mean, we're nicer to each other than we would be at school. Ben, for instance. At any school in the Southern Hemisphere Ben would be given a hard time. He stands out as a prawnhead; you can pick him out from a hundred metres. But we're quite good to him, we talk to him when he stands still long enough and no-one gives him too hard a time, even if he thinks we do.

For once I am tired tonight. Maybe it's all that fresh air with Marj. But I think I will be able to get some sleep. Might as well try anyway.

three

I THINK CHECKERS missed his mother. He wasn't that young but I think he still needed her warm tummy to cuddle into, to nuzzle his soft head against. I put him in the laundry, in a cardboard carton padded with a couple of towels I stole from the linen press. Mum and Dad had gone to bed. Dad was disgusting and for once Mum was pretty wonky. We had to come home in a taxi, and it was quite dangerous, with Dad's drunken burbles about the contract, and Mark and me and even Mum trying to shut him up. I'm not sure how much the taxidriver knew about finance, but we'd had it drummed into us from the days of rusk sticks and Play-Doh that we must never never say anything outside the family. That's why we hadn't needed Jack's lecture.

The best I could do in the cab was to get Dad talking about birthday presents again.

"What do you want?" he kept asking me in a sad old voice, as though he were on his deathbed. "What is it you want? Go on, say it. Say anything."

I tried to joke him along.

"An *A* in every subject."

"No, go on, don't be funny. You're always funny. Say something you really want. Go on."

"Friends I can trust."

"No, no, you've got friends, haven't you? Oh no, say you've got friends. I want you to have friends."

I was embarrassed that the taxidriver was listening to this.

"Yes, Dad, I've got lots of friends."

"Oh good. That's good to have friends. I want you to have friends."

"OK. I'll tell you what it is that I'd really like, that money can buy."

Even though I don't think I'm as materialistic as Mark, I'm not stupid. If someone comes along and offers to buy me anything I want, I'm not going to tell him to piss off.

"Come on, come on, tell your dad what you want."

"I want us to have a farm in the country, where we can go for weekends and school holidays."

"Oh yeah," said Mark, suddenly waking up. "I could ride my bike there." Then he thought again. "Not every weekend, though. I wouldn't want to go there every weekend."

Even though Dad was totally off his face and not responsible for what he was saying, I was still curious to see how he'd react. He was trying to get some words out but as the taxi pulled up at our front door all he managed was, "Well . . ."

He said that about ten times.

He and Mum crashed and bumped and burped and swore their way to their bedroom, Mark went to his, I put Checkers in the laundry and went to mine. Not having his mother, poor Checkers yelped continuously. I was lying awake, maybe because I'd already slept for an hour or more in Jack's poolroom. Checkers's unhappy cries were like a toothache. I listened to them for half an hour, waiting for him to stop, but it seemed like he was going to whine forever. I reached the point where I couldn't stand it anymore. So up I got and padded out to the laundry.

Checkers went into a frenzy of delight when I opened the door. It was the first time that he'd shown absolute delight at the sight of me. Come to think of it, it was the first time anyone had shown absolute delight at the sight of me.

I carried him to my bed and we snuggled in together. That was the start: I had him in there every night after that. At first I smuggled him in, but after a few fights with Mum I wore her down. He slept on the foot of the bed, wriggling himself up further as the night wore on. I had to learn to sleep with my legs folded. By halfway through the night he'd have worked his way to the middle of the bed and I'd wake all cold and bent up, and I'd start pushing Checkers back down to the end. He was so heavy to push. He wouldn't cooperate at all. He got quite grumpy about it sometimes. It was like pushing a dead body.

I miss him now. It's so lonely in this bed. Maybe it's not so good having your own room. Oliver's gone home on weekend leave and there's no-one here I want to talk to. The place is half deserted. Ben's here, but he's spending all his time talking to the old people. They're the only ones who have the patience to put up with him. Cindy's here but she just watches TV. Dreaming other people's dreams. And the only other one's Esther, but she's so drugged out at the moment she's over the Himalayas and still drifting.

So I've spent my time wandering and sitting and watching, and smoking more than I should. I wish I could think straight. My mind gets hold of something and goes over it and over it, pulling at it and tearing at it until I think I'll end up as mad as Esther. It's not always things that have actually happened; sometimes it's things that I wish had happened or that I'm scared might have happened. Tonight, before I started writing in this, it was me confronting Jack. It was so real I could smell it: I saw the veins in his face, around the nose, and I saw the anger in his transparent blue eyes.

I was sitting at one of the wrought iron tables outside Sebastian's, sipping a hot chocolate, when he suddenly appeared, dropping heavily into the seat opposite me. I burned red but didn't speak.

"Well, young lady," he said. "I hope you're satisfied with what you've done."

I still didn't say anything.

"Or is there some more damage you think you can inflict? More lives you can wreck?"

"It wasn't my fault," I said.

"Oh? That's an interesting theory. You're not a six-year-old, you know. You are responsible for what you say and do. You might like to pretend you're a child, but I've got news for you."

"That's not news."

"And you're not mentally retarded. At least I didn't think you were. Maybe I was wrong about that."

Silence.

"Was I wrong? Are you mentally retarded?"

"People don't use the word 'retarded' anymore."

"Oh, I'm sorry. I'm not politically correct enough, is that the problem? Well, let me tell you something, young lady, I've never been politically correct. I wouldn't have got where I am if I'd been worried about that bullshit."

"Yes, and look where you are."

"If it hadn't been for you, there'd never have been a problem."

"There was a problem long before I came along."

And suddenly, according to my imagination, I'd be on my feet, screaming, "Why didn't you leave us alone? Why did you have to drag us in? You're scum, filth. I hate you. Go away. You deserve everything, everything, you understand? Everything that you get. It's not my fault. IT'S NOT MY FAULT."

It was so real I was trembling. None of it happened of course. But for hours, while Cindy gazed at the TV, I watched this movie in my head, running it over and over, changing the dialogue each time, trying to find words I could say to him that would be more powerful, more effective.

I'd actually had a few hot chocolates with him at Sebastian's over the years. Rosie went shopping in Lisle Street every Saturday morning and Jack sometimes went with her. But he got bored quickly and started looking for someone to talk to, someone to entertain him. Three or four times I was that person. I liked it; it made me feel quite grown-up. Heads turned as we sat down; people pretended not to be impressed by the fact that he was sitting a couple of metres from them; waiters were faster, smoother, oilier than they ever were for me alone. I copped the power of Jack at its full blast on those occasions, and understood a little how Dad could have become so completely at his beck and call. But I still resented them both: Jack for making it happen and Dad for allowing it.

Now that I'm writing about it, I've calmed down a bit. That's good. I was in full panic attack mode in the TV Room, and trying desperately not to let the staff see. I don't want to have my drugs increased again. I want so much to be able to do it on my own, and in this place I don't think I'll get that chance. I'll end up like Esther, a spaced-out koala, staring at people as though I'm in the zoo, up the top of my gum tree and off my face on eucalyptus.

I took a pause then and got out of bed and went to the window. There's not much to see from here but I like it OK. At night I think of it as an ocean, with islands between this building and the road, a hundred metres away. There are half a dozen islands, each one created by a spotlight. The lights are pretty strong: you can see every blade of grass, looking dry and lifeless in the glare. But outside the pools of light it's all dark, like the ocean, black and secret. To reach the road, oh, to reach that road, that strip of life with its busy whizzing cars, with normal people rushing through their lives . . . that's our aim. The life that we once lived so easily, so effortlessly. We lived it like we breathed it—in, out; in, out—not knowing that the time would come when every movement of our lives would be an effort, when we'd have to think about every step, every word, every gesture. Nothing's unconscious for me now, everything's self-conscious.

There are some things that once you've lost, you never get back. Innocence is one. Love is another. I guess childhood is a third. I've lost all of those, these last few months. I don't know how to replace them. I don't know if there is anything that can replace them.

four

CHECKERS AND I WATCHED television together the day the contract was announced. Checkers had grown into a four-legged lunatic. He just lived to party. While I was watching TV, Checkers was watching me, hoping I'd start something—preferably a fight. His favourite activities were walks and eats, but fights came a close third. To start one, all it took was for me to grab his snout and hold his mouth shut for a while. The moment I released him, Checkers would leap away and come back with eyes flashing and jaws snapping and spit flying. If I wouldn't play, he'd stretch out his front legs and drop his head, then, with his bum up in the air and his tail wagging like a metronome, he'd bark and bark.

If I did keep it going we'd roll around the floor like wrestlers, me grabbing for his nose and Checkers snapping at my hands. He had amazing timing. Not once did he bite me. He'd often catch my hand and hold it in his teeth as I tried to get it back but he never broke my skin, never spilt my blood.

That's more than I can say for Mark.

We used to fight so much. Bloody noses, corked arms: he even broke my finger once. The last year I started beating him, though: he wasn't so keen then.

When he—Checkers, that is—was little his teeth were like rows of needles. They were so sharp! He was a canine acupuncturist. When he held my hand then, I'd end up with red dots all over my skin from those little sharp points.

But the day we watched the contract being announced Checkers just had to lie there depressed, because I wanted to see Dad and the others looking beautiful for the cameras. I saw it on two different news programmes and two current affairs shows before I got bored: it was the same sort of stuff on each one. No-one else was home: Mum had gone into the city to join Dad for another celebration—the official one this time—and Mark was at Josh's. So there was no-one to share it with, no-one to see how I felt, no-one to talk to about what it was like to sit on the floor and watch Jack lie so publicly, so professionally.

"What were your impressions of the tendering process?"

"Very fair, very thorough."

"How did you feel when you found out you'd won?"

"Well, terrific, as you can imagine. We've been celebrating all day, and we'll be celebrating tonight too, I can tell you. But tomorrow, tomorrow we'll be straight down to work, planning stage one."

"Is this contract just a licence to print money?"

"Oh no! No way! Who have you been talking to? This is an enterprise like any other. It could succeed and it could fail. Obviously it's our assessment that we can make the project viable at our tender, but we'll have to work very hard to ensure that it's a success."

"How much did Rider Group tender?"

"Well, that's still a confidential matter, as you'd appreciate. It's a question of the commercial sensitivity of the figures."

"What do you think gave Rider Group the edge?"

"Obviously price is the big factor. But the Commission was authorised to take other aspects into account, such as the quality of the design and what it would contribute to the city, the level of offshore investment and the integrity of the tendering company. I'd like to think that we came out well on all those counts."

Dad only spoke on one of the shows. On *Tickertape* he and Jack were interviewed, and Dad talked about the share prices and the level of debt to equity, stuff like that. Because it's a financial show they got into the kind of heavy details that I don't really understand. It's when *Tickertape* finished that I switched off the TV.

As soon as I did, Checkers's head came up eagerly and he looked at me with wild hope. So I teased him a bit, walking casually towards the front door, but not saying the magic word, the word he was sweating on. He followed eagerly, almost on tiptoes, quivering with optimism, till I felt sorry for him and said it.

"WALK."

Then, as always, it was a matter of getting the door

open so that this yelping, turbocharged, hysterical mutt could explode onto the park, scattering birds, leaves, puddles and other dogs.

I loved the joy Checkers had. The way he rushed at life. If he'd been a high diver he would have run to the end of every board and leapt off with tail wagging, barking enthusiastically, soaring through the air, sniffing all the way down, not caring what he'd find at the bottom till he arrived. That was the way he approached everything.

The park was so lush and full of life, compared to these hospital grounds anyway. It's something to do with the kind of world I've always lived in, I think, that I'm used to things being lush and rich and perfect. Luncheons are always beautifully arranged on elegant plates, bathrooms are always white marble with huge black towels, people never slop around with their hair in rollers and their feet in carpet slippers.

The park had beds of crocuses and daffodils, stuff like that. Rhododendrons. A special rose garden.

The hospital grounds could have been grassy and flowery too, but no-one had taken the trouble. When Marj tried, we didn't give her much support.

No-one else at the hospital had taken much trouble with anything. They'd painted the corridors off-white and light brown, but they hadn't repainted them for quite a while. Near the nurses' station there's a notice-board with posters about AIDS and smoking and breast cancer and cheerful stuff like that. Guaranteed to brighten up the lives of the psychotics, the demented and the terminally depressed. There are four postcards too, from staff on holidays, and three thank-you cards from ex-patients. I smiled to myself when I heard Oliver and Daniel talking one day, and realised that we all knew all seven cards by heart: we'd read them so many times, waiting for our medication.

Along from the noticeboard is a bunch of artwork done by previous patients of the Adolescent Unit. They're sort of posters, a bit like CD covers, all pretty aggro and heavy metal, except for one that's more gothic. Most of them are full of knives and blood and stuff, with slogans like "School Sux," and I think they're there to show new admissions to the Adolescent Unit what a trendy cool place it is. Marj denies that, of course, but it's what I think.

There's nothing else in the corridor, and nothing special in the wards either, except for a painting in each one. Like I said, in mine it's a picture of a dog by a fire.

Yes, no-one's taken much trouble with things. Some of the staff take trouble with people, but no-one takes much trouble with things. Marj planting trees is about the only exception.

I feel sad to think that a day of my life has passed the way today did, with so little happening, nothing being achieved. I've been alive for 5,675 days, which is quite a lot, but I still don't feel good about wasting any of them. Today really was hopeless. We had school this morning, or baby-sitting, as Daniel calls it. I'm sure they gave Mr Coe the job here because he couldn't handle a regular class in a school and someone at the Education

Department thought he should at least be able to handle a small group in a hospital. But he can't handle us. A class of seven shouldn't be much of a problem, but then we're a pretty weird class. Cindy's so rude to him, Ben pesters him with questions, Oliver just does whatever he feels like. Daniel and Esther and Emine and I, the ones who've been here the longest, are meant to be doing correspondence, but Esther spends her whole time looking at art books.

I finished a Maths assignment this morning. That's something, I suppose, but I went there determined that I'd do at least three assignments. I just frittered the hours away, listening to Oliver and Cindy swapping jokes and goss, feeling a bit jealous maybe.

Then Mr Coe put on a video of *Macbeth* for Emine, and I was half watching that. So the morning dawdled off into the distance.

Lunch was a watery chicken noodle soup, then chicken and macaroni. Bad day for chickens. Then we had Group and Marj got angry at Daniel for mucking around and not taking things seriously. She keeps using the word "work" for what we're doing. "You worked well today." "There's a lot of work to be done on that yet." "We've been working on this for quite a while." I don't know if it's work. I don't think it's what my father, or Jack, would call work.

We were meant to be focussing on Ben, but we didn't get far. Cindy was hopeless: when we're not talking about her she's not interested. Esther was slumped in a chair. I don't think they've got her medication right yet.

Normally it's Oliver and Daniel and Emine who do the "work," but today only Oliver seemed willing to put much in. Of course Ben was nervous as hell, all over the place, like he always is when the pressure's on him. He wouldn't say much about his family—he never does—but he talked about his school.

"They're all such dickheads there. I hate them."

"Why do you hate them, Ben?" Marj asked.

"I don't know. They're just real wankers. All they ever talk about is what they want to do with girls, and stuff like that. They're so boring."

"Don't you have any friends, Ben?" said Cindy, as if she didn't care whether he did or not—or worse, as if she already knew he didn't and despised him for it.

"Yeah, of course."

"So what's your problem?" Oliver asked.

"I don't know. I didn't ask to come here."

"How have you all found Ben in your time here?" Marj asked. "Daniel, why don't you start? How do you find Ben?"

"I just look around and there he is," Daniel said, laughing hysterically at his hilarious joke.

No-one else bothered. Marj was as patient as ever. She just waited, looking at Daniel, till he got the message and calmed down.

"Daniel?" she said again.

"Oh well, you know. He's a bit selfish sometimes. But I don't mind him. He doesn't bother me."

There was a long boring discussion then about Ben being selfish. It was mainly about how he won't let anyone change channels on the TV, which is an annoying habit of Ben's, but no worse than anyone else's annoying habits.

"Cindy, how do you find Ben?"

"He's a cool guy. He's really funny."

This was so obviously a lie, but no-one called Cindy on it. She just said it because she was too lazy to say anything else.

"Emine?"

"Well, I think Ben's kind of sweet?" Emine says everything like she's asking a question. "He's always nice to me, you know? But I don't know, I feel sorry for him sometimes. He doesn't seem to have many friends? He seems kind of lonely?"

"Why do you think that's so?"

"Well, I don't know exactly. He's just different to everyone else."

"Everybody's different to everybody else," said Daniel.

"Oh really?" said Cindy. "What I want to know is, why can't we smoke in Group?"

"Cindy," said Marj, "I understand that you're feeling resentful and angry today, but I'm going to ask you to be patient for a little while longer, till we finish looking at ways we can help support Ben."

That's the way they all talk in here.

"Oliver, how do you feel about Ben?" Marj asked then.

"I like him but he drives me crazy."

Marj started salivating. She loves comments like that.

"You find him irritating?"

"Yeah. Look, Ben, what I want to know is why don't

you just sit down and talk properly, like normal people? It's like the moment we start talking, you've got to go somewhere. Are you on something, or what?"

"We're all on something in here," Daniel said.

"It's because I'm attention deficit hyperactive," said Ben.

"Say what?" said Cindy, who always tries to sound American.

"And what the hell is that when it's awake?" Daniel asked.

"Talk English," Oliver said.

Marj interrupted. "It's true that Ben has been diagnosed as attention deficit hyperactive," she said. "That does account for some of his restlessness. But there's a lot more to your problems than that, Ben, as you know—and I don't think we can dismiss everything as being a result of the syndrome. Now, Oliver, you were saying?"

"Oh well," said Oliver, "it's just that he seems so damn nervous all the time. You can't have a proper conversation with him because he never seems to want to talk about anything for more than thirty seconds. And when we're playing basketball, like, two on two, he keeps mucking around and stealing the ball and stuff. Like last night, Ben, you went for that two-hundred-metre dribble right around the carpark. You thought it was pretty funny . . ."

"It was," said Ben, giggling and squirming with delight as he remembered his moment of glory.

"Yeah, for you maybe, but not for everyone else. And

even when we all got mad and were yelling at you, you still wouldn't bring it back."

Ben was trying to stop giggling, but not because he felt embarrassed at being so juvenile, only because he knew he'd get in more trouble with us if he didn't shut up fast.

That's what I mean. Discussing Ben taking the basketball was the most important achievement of the whole day. It's so frustrating. I can't stand it sometimes. I was in quite a good mood last night, but today was kind of marginal.

five

THINGS WENT ALONG so calmly for so long. I copped a lot of envy from other girls: they didn't say much but I saw it in their eyes. When they did say anything it was usually as a joke, like "Oh, you can afford it," or "Does your father want a personal assistant?"

We hardly ever saw Dad. He'd always worked hard; now he doubled it. He took to going to the office at five o'clock in the mornings. He said he got more done then, because no-one else was in and there were no phone calls. But he worked late into the evenings as well. The subject of our presents didn't come up again for quite a while, although it was sort of understood that Mark would get his motorbike. No-one mentioned my idea at all. I thought it was actually a seriously good one. We could all be together in the country, having picnics under trees, swimming in the river, riding horses, everyone happy. But maybe they thought it was just some dumb teenage spur-of-the-moment junk. Probably

Dad had been so pissed that night he'd forgotten it. I couldn't be bothered bringing it up again.

Apart from Dad working the much longer hours, I didn't see much change in our lives. It wasn't what I'd expected. At one stage I thought that we'd be living in total luxury, in some huge mansion where we wouldn't have to do any work, just lie by the pool all day drinking from golden goblets. But no, it wasn't like that.

Oh, Checkers, he was the other big change of course. Not always for the good either—I mean, he caused heaps of trouble. Our neighbours—well, the Sykeses weren't a problem but the Whites hated him, right from the start. They complained every chance they got. And Checkers seemed to sense that. How else could you explain the way he acted around them? And having no fence between the houses meant he could cause a lot of aggravation. Whenever Checkers wanted a crap he went to their back lawn. It was like he saved it all up for their place. He never crapped anywhere else. And, to save aggravation, I used to go and shovel it up and bury it. I hated that job. *Really* hated it, I mean; not just the way people say "Oh I hate doing that," and giggle. It made me sick to my stomach. Those moist little heaps, different shades of brown, the fresh ones still glistening, the older ones drier and darker—see, I can make myself sick just by writing about them.

I could never be a mother because I could never bring myself to change the nappies.

Anyway, Checkers. Some of the things he did to the Whites were quite legendary. They had a cat, Muggins, stupid ugly big thing that was a sort of purple colour. It looked like the hair on an old lady after she'd had it dyed. No, I'm exaggerating. It was a blue-grey colour and could trace its ancestry back to Henry the Second or someone. Of course Checkers, who had a bit of hunting blood in him (I think he was part cocker spaniel), thought that Muggins was provided purely for his amusement, or to keep him in practice. He spent half his life chasing Muggins, who had to change from a ground dweller to a tree dweller if he wanted to stay alive. Mark and I made things worse by deliberately sooling Checkers onto Muggins whenever the Whites went out and we saw their heap of purple fluff prowling round the place. It got so that all we had to do was say, "Muggins, Checkers, Muggins," and he would detonate into a frenzy of barks, rushing around looking for a victim to tear limb from limb.

One afternoon I was in the garden studying for a Biol test when I saw a movement out of the corner of my eye. I looked up in time to see a streak of blue-grey doing about one-fifty across the lawn. Checkers was in hot pursuit, siren wailing and lights flashing. Muggins skidded around the corner of the Whites' pool, raced along the end section, turned again and made for the gazebo. Checkers, seeing where he was headed, decided to go for the shortcut and took a flying leap across the pool. He got about a third of the way over before belly-flopping in a great splash of spray. But he wasn't bothered. He paddled forward bravely, looking for the cat. Only problem was that when he got to the other side he couldn't get out; I had to leave the Biol books and go and rescue him.

It was only a week later that the Whites were at our place for a tennis party. Everyone was sitting around being very elegant: "No, really, you go on, I've just had a set . . . ," "Isn't she marvellous . . . ," "Oh, well played, partner . . . ," "Let me get you a drink, darling, you've certainly earned it . . ." Mark was there, scabbing a cake, but we weren't allowed to play: it was an adult party. Suddenly a strange cat, a reddish-coloured one, trotted down the drive and leapt onto the little wall beside the garage. Without thinking Mark yelled out, "Muggins, Checkers, Muggins."

Like a ground-to-air missile, Checkers launched himself straight at the Whites' place. He didn't even see the visiting cat, although the cat saw Checkers and was gone in a blur of orange.

A second after he'd yelled out, Mark realised what he'd done. By then it was too late, of course. Mr and Mrs White were seriously angry. "Well, really," Mrs White said, standing up. "June," said Mr White, turning to my mother, "this is the bloody limit. These kids have got no respect for anything. They just do as they like."

My mother started falling apart. You get to recognise the symptoms if you've seen them often enough: the trembling lower lip, the head dropping, having to lean on something with both hands. Normally Mrs White was pretty sympathetic when Mum couldn't cope—Mrs White always blamed Dad—but this time she was too fired up to be sympathetic. Mark and I had to stand there, with our heads down too, while we got told what irresponsible, immature, untrustworthy little criminals we were.

I wished Mum would stick up for us at times like this, but she never once did. It was the same when we were in trouble at school. She wanted everything to be so perfect: tennis parties, her children, the appearance of the house, herself. She went into instant spinout when they weren't. Sometimes it seemed with me she was spinning out all the time, because I was never perfect, not once, ever.

Anyway, the tennis party struggled on. Mark and I had to apologise, Checkers was tied up, and the conversation, from what I heard of it, got very lame. It was a long time before the Whites spoke to Mark or me again.

But it was a typical episode from life with Checkers. Where he was, nothing was predictable or dull or in a rut. That's one reason I'd love to have him with me now, in here. This place is so predictable. They need a Checkers to brighten them up—staff and patients both. It's funny, because all of the patients are weird in their own special ways. Apart from Ben with his attention deficit hyperactivity, there's Oliver with his eating disorder, Emine with school phobia, Cindy who tried to kill herself, Daniel with an obsessive-compulsive disorder, and Esther who's "query psychotic," according to Sister Llosa, when I heard them discussing the patients at the change of shifts one day. I think that means they're not sure whether she's totally off her board, or just normal average crazy like the rest of us.

In a way, though, Daniel seems the most crazy. I don't know how an obsessive-compulsive disorder works, but there's something quite funny about it to people like me, who haven't got it. The strange thing—or one of the strange things—is that Daniel can laugh at it, too. He actually laughs at the weird stuff he does, but he can't stop himself doing it. For instance, one of his obsessions is with cleanliness. Like my mum, only worse. He spends four, five, six hours a day in the shower. This causes problems for some of the staff, like Sister Norman, who's obsessed with the fact that Daniel is gay and gets nervous when any guys are in the bathroom too long with him. She goes around looking for male nurses she can send in to check out the situation, and if she can't find any she sails in there herself. The more paranoid she gets, the more Daniel teases her. When someone who's in on the joke, Oliver for example, is in the bathroom Daniel drops all the pickup lines he can think of, in a loud voice, while Sister Norman goes into a frenzy outside. She knows Daniel's just stirring her but she can never be quite sure, and it drives her crazy: the steam floating out of the bathroom and, with it, Daniel's voice: "Oliver, that's such a big one . . . wow, look at that . . ."

Daniel spends so much time in the shower he gets all pink and wrinkly. But his obsession with cleanliness isn't just to do with taking showers. A couple of days ago he lost ten bucks and, about two minutes after I heard him complaining about it, I saw the money blowing along the driveway near the basketball court. I chased it, grabbed it and took it in to the Dayroom and tried to give it to him. He took one look and backed away fast.

"What's wrong?" I asked.

"Where'd you find it?" he asked suspiciously.

"Outside," I said. "Blowing down the drive, across from the court."

"I can't touch it," he said.

"You're kidding."

"I wish I was. But I can't, not when it's been contaminated like that. Listen, if you want to do me a really big favour, change it for a new one on Wednesday, when the bank comes. Then I'll be able to have it back."

It was weird. I can't imagine living like that. That's why Daniel never plays basketball, of course. In fact he spends most of his time indoors.

He's got other obsessions too, not all related to cleanliness. He won't go into a new room until he's touched five different types of wood. He said it started with the saying "touch wood," and he got in the habit of touching wood before any new experience, then he figured that the more different types of wood he touched, the more lucky he'd be.

He gets dressed in a certain order, even buttoning up his shirt by doing alternate buttons, starting at the bottom, then going back down.

Like I say, I don't know how he survives. I don't know how he gets anything done in life.

Somehow, though, despite the individual weirdnesses of the people in here, when you put them together the effect is dullsville. I don't know whether it's the staff or the drugs or the monotony of the daily routine, or all those things. Maybe every institution is like this. But it sure is getting on my nerves.

I suppose that's the ultimate joke. We're here because of our nerves and the place makes us worse. Some joke, some catch.

"Yossarian was moved very deeply by the absolute simplicity of this clause of Catch-22, and let out a respectful whistle. 'That's some catch, that Catch-22,' he observed.

"'It's the best there is,' Doc Daneeka agreed."

I love that book. But we could teach the guys in *Catch-22* a thing or two.

six

MY LIFE SEEMED to fall apart so quickly. I don't suppose it was that quick really; it just felt that way. The first hint of trouble came when I was reading the paper one day in the school library. I don't often read the paper but I was skipping History and I'd told Miss Mackay, the Librarian, that I was there to do an Issues essay for English. So looking at the newspaper seemed to be the best camouflage, even if I'd just planned to read the star signs and *Far Side*.

But when I got to page five I saw the name "Rider" in the headline, so I stopped to have a look. It was a name I was used to seeing in the paper: usually in the financial pages, but not always. Jack kind of attracted cameras and reporters. He didn't give a damn what anyone thought, so that meant he did some radical things. A lot of them really upset me, like the time he demolished the old house where Frank Langston used to live. Jack knocked it down before the Langston Society could take out a preservation order. Typical.

This story was about the casino, of course. An Opposition member of Parliament was asking questions about Rider Group and the contract. She said that there was a sudden rise in share prices two months before the contract was announced. So she asked the minister, "Were the directors of Rider Group engaged in trading the company's shares in early June? Did they have prior knowledge that they had been successful in their tender for the casino? If so, how could such knowledge have been obtained?"

In reply the minister accused the member of being on a fishing expedition. He said the Government had monitored the tendering process closely from its inception and was totally satisfied with the confidentiality of the Commission. The member's attitude was typical of the Opposition, who skulked around in the shadows trying to find corpses where no corpses existed. They would serve the people of this state better if they tried to do something constructive once in a while.

And that was pretty much all the newspaper said. Most people reading it would probably have thought that was the end of the matter. Not for me, though. I felt my face go red as I sat there, and the sweat prickled my skin. It was obvious what had happened. Once they knew they'd got the contract they'd gone out and loaded up on shares. I don't know a heap about the stock market but I know that's illegal. It's called insider trading.

Still, I wasn't totally blown away about it. I knew there were always things going on that you wouldn't necessarily want to read about in the newspapers. Not just with Rider Group. It must be the same with any big company, surely. And there had been controversies with Rider Group before. I had a lot of faith in Jack being smart enough to navigate through any storm. Jack and my father.

As it turned out, though, this controversy went on a bit longer than most. The next day there was a report that the Stock Exchange had asked Rider Group to explain the rise in its share prices in June and to provide information about any trading in company shares by its directors for that month. And, the next day, Dad issued a statement saying that all dealings by directors had at all times been honest and aboveboard, that the company had nothing to hide and would cooperate fully with any requests for information from the Stock Exchange.

Then it was the weekend. Saturday morning I had breakfast with Dad and he was pretty relaxed. “Look, it’s nothing,” he said. “Just a backbencher trying to make a name for herself, and Leslie Croft trying to prove that he’s worth all the money the Stock Exchange pays him.”

Sunday we went to Jack and Rosie’s for a barbeque. Jack was even redder in the face and louder than normal, putting his arm around everyone and breathing fumes of Scotch into their faces. Everything seemed larger than life that day. The jokes were louder, the laughter longer. Everyone seemed to be shouting. Then Mark came out to the garden, from the TV room. “There’s something going to be on TV in a minute,” he said, “about Rider Group.”

“Yeah?” Jack said. “What?”

"I don't know," Mark said. "Something about a company in the Bahamas."

Without a word Jack went inside. We all followed. No-one said anything. There were no kids in the TV room, just a man's face on the screen talking to the empty room.

". . . kind of animal would do that?" he asked. "Rip off an old-age pensioner by preying on her worst fears. It makes you wonder, doesn't it? Next, Laura Bailey's exclusive story about the mystery company in the Bahamas who's bought a slice of one of our biggest corporations."

The ads ran their course, and still no-one spoke. I kept looking from Jack to Dad and back again. Dad looked nervous, but it was impossible to tell with Jack. He stood there holding his drink, glaring at the TV. I suppose his tight grip on the glass was the only clue that he was not completely relaxed.

Finally the ads finished and the man came back on. I knew the programme—it was *Max Locke's Spotlight,* but Max must have been on holidays. I didn't know who this guy was. He said something like, "And now a *Spotlight* exclusive: Laura Bailey reports on a mystery company in the Bahamas that's been buying up big in Rider Group. Who are the secret investors who already own a good slice of our newest casino?"

Then they crossed to the reporter, who was standing on a beach somewhere. It was meant to be the Bahamas but it could just as easily have been Bondi. She launched into her story. What it boiled down to was that a shelf company called Pinto, with a paid-up capital of two dollars, had bought about eight percent of Rider—and had done it in four days in June. The company had only two directors, a Mr and Mrs Wills. There was a couple of minutes of video of a man and a woman on a veranda and then in the garden of a white mansion. You could only see blurry figures, glimpses of them through the trees. Laura Bailey's voice told us that the Willses were a British couple who had lived there for eleven years and were listed on the census forms as investors. That was all there was to it really. They'd managed to stretch thirty seconds' worth of information into a four-minute story.

When it was over Jack just shrugged. "Not much in that," he said to Dad, who nodded.

"What's it all about?" Mark asked.

"It's a company that's bought some Rider Group shares," Dad explained. "We've been wondering about them ourselves, but that story didn't tell us much that we didn't already know."

We went back outside to the barbeque, but the party had quietened down, and everyone went home early.

So, that was how it all began. A few questions in Parliament, a story on TV. Now, as I lie here, it feels like my whole world has shrunk to this little bed. From living in the big house, where we had the pool and the court and all those downstairs rooms, to this tiny house of white, with its light blue bedspread. When I sleep, which isn't very often—even with the tablets—I get right down under the sheets, pulling them over my head. The air gets a bit stale but I feel safer, more secure, doing that. It's my white cocoon where I can be a caterpillar, a grub, never to turn into a butterfly or even a moth. It's the safest place I know. It's the only time and the only place where I can feel some peace.

seven

No matter how hard I try, I'm still fooled by appearances. I know it's wrong but I still fall for them. Whether it's a good-looking boy who I think must be really nice, or a drunk whom I cross the street to avoid, or an old lady who I take for granted must be conservative and old-fashioned.

I thought Esther was crazy, the way she hums to herself and walks in patterns, the way she collects bits of string and ties them together in a long rope, her endless questions to the kitchen staff about the food they're serving. Well, she may be crazy but at least she's interesting and intelligent. I realise that now, after talking to her for hours tonight. We started talking in the bathroom. When I went to wash my hands, standing next to her, I realised she was trying to slip a piece of paper under a silverfish that was scurrying around in the handbasin.

"What are you doing?" I asked. It was the first time

I've ever spoken directly to her. I don't talk to anyone here much, except Oliver.

"Saving its life," she said. And laughed.

"Saving its life? Why bother?"

"Why would I want it to die?"

I just looked at her and she laughed again. Laughter's not a sound we hear a lot in this place, and Esther's laugh is quite nice.

"It's such a complex little creature," she said. "So delicate. Imagine how long it'd take to make one, if you were a human insect-maker. You could spend your whole life working on it and still not get even one finished. And we kill them so casually. A quick squish of the finger and a moment later we've forgotten that we did it."

I started to feel guilty. "Is that why you're so fussy about what you eat?"

"Mmm."

We got talking about everything then. I leant against the wall for a while, then gradually slid down till I was sitting on the cold white tiled floor. Opposite me, Esther did the same. When we got too cold we moved out to the corridor and went down past the staircase, where there's a little dead end with a dried-out palm in a pot. We settled there quite comfortably. Esther did most of the talking. She was very interesting. She lives in Sanford but she doesn't go to school, never has. She is a "home schooler," something I never heard of before. It means she does school by correspondence, with her parents helping. They live on a half-hectare block and grow their own vegetables organically and keep chooks and make their own bread and annoy the neighbours. I guess they would, in Sanford. It's not exactly a suburb filled with hippies—which is what they are, in some ways.

Then everything went wrong. Her mother got sick, really sick, with cancer of the uterus, and she had to spend long periods in hospital. When she wasn't in hospital she was away in the mountains, or even interstate, trying different cures, natural therapies and stuff. For about fifteen months she wasn't around much, and Esther's father couldn't cope with that, because he depended on her pretty heavily. So he spent most of his time at his mum's place in the country, having a nervous breakdown.

He wanted Esther to come with him but she wouldn't. For one thing she wanted to be able to visit her mum in hospital; for another she felt she had to look after the chooks and the garden; for a third she doesn't like her grandmother.

So, for weeks on end, Esther was there alone. "I liked it," she said, "but I think I did go a bit crazy."

"How do you mean?" I asked. I was fascinated. There was no-one at my school who lived like this.

"Oh well." She looked at me for a minute, as if working out what she should say. She's very beautiful, Esther, like a gypsy, with long ringlets framing her dark face, and deep eyes. She always wears orangey-browny-earthy things, and lots of silver jewellery. I've never actually met or seen a gypsy, but I imagine that's how they look.

Finally she decided. "I think I have an animal in my head," she confessed.

"An animal?" I was shocked, but I wanted to laugh.

"Yes. I know it's crazy—at least, I think I do—but that's why I'm in here."

"What kind of animal?"

"Well . . . I'm not sure exactly. A little warm furry one, like a possum or a feather-tail glider."

"Um, that does sound pretty weird," I said, immediately trying to bite the end off my tongue for saying something so dumb. I was scared that Esther would go into a frenzied fit, foaming at the mouth and trying to kill me.

But she just smiled and said, "Exactly!"

"What's it like?" I asked. "Having it in there, I mean."

"It's quite nice, really. It probably sounds terrible. But I just feel that it's there, curled up all warm and nice."

I didn't say anything. I was trying to imagine how it would be.

"Sometimes it moves," Esther added, "and I feel that, feel it wriggling around, squirming into a new position, to get more comfortable. And sometimes it makes noises."

"Noises?"

"Mmm. Sort of whimpery noises. Little yelps and cries. I guess it's the noises that put me in here."

"They did?"

I gulped. I was scared I was getting in too deep.

"Mmm. The neighbours heard the noises and they

called the cops. You see, I guess the noises must have been coming out of my mouth."

"Uh-huh."

She laughed. "Don't worry. I know I sound like I'm totally out of my tree, and I probably am, but you look like you're expecting me to jump up at any moment and attack you with a pair of scissors."

It was exactly what I had been thinking.

"What happened with your mother and the cancer?" I asked.

"She's fine. She's in remission, has been for a while now. But Dad's still living with his mum. I don't know when he'll be coming back. I don't know if he'll be coming back at all."

We sat there talking till Hanna came along and shooed us off to our rooms so she could turn the lights out. This place is so hung up on routine—meals, medication, Group, bedtime—everything's got to be at the exact time or the world will fall off its axis and we'll all be thrown into space.

So now I'm lying awake thinking about Esther. It was good to talk to her; easier than talking to almost anyone I can name, except maybe Oliver. I don't know why I was so relaxed. You wouldn't usually choose to have a conversation with someone who thinks she's got an animal in her head. I still didn't say much when I was with her, but I felt comfortable.

I think it's because she didn't seem like she was ready to criticise, to judge me and find me guilty every chance she got. That's the way a lot of people have always seemed to me, including some of my so-called friends from school. Girls like Shon. The day I said Kylie Becker was my favourite singer—and I still do like her—God, it was like I'd committed social suicide. Shon didn't let me forget that for a month. Just because I didn't choose someone they'd decided was cool. It made me wonder if I was allowed to have my own opinion on anything.

I've always been like that—afraid of doing the wrong thing, of making a fool of myself—but it's been a thousand percent worse since everything happened with Rider Group. I've written about some of that already of course. The first things that went wrong weren't my fault, nothing to do with me. That company in the Bahamas, that was the first problem. And Mrs O'Shea, the Opposition backbencher asking questions in Parliament: she made her reputation out of Rider Group. She's a shadow minister now.

But again, that wasn't me. How could it be? I didn't know what was going on.

In fact after the TV show things quietened down again. I'd almost forgotten about it by the time the next wave came. It was a monster wave, though, a dumper. I opened the paper one morning to get the TV guide. Dad had gone to work early again, Mark was having breakfast with me, Mum wasn't up yet. And all across the front page was Rider Group. We were bigger than royal divorces. I choked on my Coco Pops and suddenly couldn't eat any more. I had a horrible feeling that things were getting out of control. I read the front page and the continuation of the story on pages six and seven, trying to hide it from Mark. There were three main points. One was that over the last four months the company in the Bahamas had sent two million dollars to a company in London. And among the directors of that company were Mum, and Jack's wife Rosie.

The second point came from a document supposedly leaked from the Commission. It was a handwritten note that the newspaper said was in the Deputy Chairman's writing. It said: "Rudi rang again, insisted it must be R., said P. was 'waiting impatiently' on our decision."

This wouldn't have meant anything to me, but the newspaper helpfully translated it. They said Rudi was Rudi Koneckny, a researcher on the Premier's personal staff. They suggested P. was the Premier himself, and R. was Rider Group. And they made it pretty clear that if they were right about that, there would be shit flying round in a big way. The Premier had always been so definite that he wouldn't be involved in the selection process, that it had to be totally impartial, independent, honest.

The third point was that the other two main bidders for the contract were claiming that their bids were higher than Rider Group's but, as the Commission, the Government and Jack were all refusing to say how much the winning bid was, it was hard to tell whether that story was true or not.

I took the paper into Mum. Her head was somewhere under the pillows. I threw the paper at her and said, "There's some nice news to wake up to," and stormed off to the bus. I felt like my life was going to become complicated and bad, and I was right on both counts.

eight

By the time the six o'clock news rolled around everyone had his story ready. The Premier said that Mr Koneckny had assured him there was no truth in the morning newspaper's report and he himself had not interfered with the tendering process in any way. He had met Jack only a couple of times at social functions, the last one of which was the Derby two years before, and he had never met Dad. The story was just another media beat-up, and typical of the *Advocate*'s bias against the Government. The Deputy Chairman of the Commission said he had never been approached by Mr Koneckny in a manner that could be seen as prejudicial to the Commission's proceedings; the Commission's deliberations had at all times remained confidential and impartial; the Commission had had no dealings with Jack or Dad apart from their appearances at the hearings. The story was just another media beat-up, and typical of the *Advocate*'s bias against the Commission.

Jack and Dad issued a joint statement saying that they had no prior knowledge, that they had at all times acted properly and that the last time Jack had spoken to the Premier was two years ago, in a crowd at the Derby. Dad had never spoken to him. The story was just another media beat-up, and typical of the *Advocate*'s bias against the business sector.

I watched it until I felt sick. Mum wasn't home, and neither was Dad of course. Mark watched it with me, but when I tried to talk to him about it he wouldn't answer, just went off to his bedroom. So I took Checkers out to the park again.

Somehow, even Checkers doing canine aerobics from one end of the park to the other didn't make me feel any better. People say dogs are sensitive to their owners' moods, but I don't think Checkers was too tuned in to mine. Or maybe he did know how nervous and depressed I was feeling, and deliberately did idiotic things to cheer me up. One thing's for sure, he was even madder than normal that day. He stole a jumper that a man had left lying on the ground while he pushed his little daughter backwards and forwards on the swing. Checkers, for no reason at all, grabbed the jumper and trotted away proudly holding it in his mouth. I gasped, then shouted: "Checkers! Bad dog! Put it down! Checkers! Come here!" The man saw what was going on, and he started chasing Checkers, who thought this was a great new game. He accelerated. For about five minutes the two of us, followed by the little kid, chased Checkers around and around. Even though his feet got tangled up in the jumper a few times, he was too fast and too smart for us. When we got close to him he showed the whites of his eyes and charged through the gap between us. Twice I touched a back leg, but I couldn't get a grip, and away he went again. I felt frustrated and embarrassed that I couldn't control him, and angry that he was making me look stupid in front of the man and his daughter.

I don't think the man was very amused. He didn't chuck a tantrum or anything—he even made a couple of half-jokes about it—but he didn't look too happy. Finally he grabbed Checkers's hindquarters as Checkers scuttled past, and we were able to wrestle the jumper out of his mouth. It had a few holes in it, but it wasn't too bad. I kept apologising and grovelling, while the little girl clung to her father's legs and looked at me like I was a serial killer. I suppose to her I was just another big scary stranger. Worse, I was a big scary stranger who owned a savage killer dog.

They went. I was too depressed to be mad at Checkers. I sat on the swing while he romped around me, trying to get me to play. After a while he gave up on me and went off and started sniffing the rubbish tins.

I sat there a long time. I had some childish idea that if I sat there long enough they'd miss me and come and look for me. They didn't, of course. After an hour or two it got so cold I had to go back. By then even Checkers was sick of the park and was lying near me, watching from under his eyelids, waiting to see when I'd make a move. It always cracked me up when he did that. His eyes looked so intelligent, peering out of that crazy checked coat.

Lately I've started to feel too safe, too comfortable in this hospital. No, not comfortable, just secure. Like I'm getting scared to leave, to go back to the outside world. The real world, everyone here calls it, as though this is an unreal world. Of course it is in a way: everyone on drugs, everyone depressed or crazy, no-one working. Even the few things here that are meant to be like the outside world—school and the kiosk and the bank—aren't like anything I've seen before.

But in some ways this world is more real than the one outside. In here the masks are off, people don't pretend so much. We still fake it when we can, but most of the time we don't have the energy or the strength. We've all hit the rocks or we wouldn't be here; when you're drowning you don't worry so much about how you look or what you say or whether you've got a nice swimming style.

I keep a mask on even here, though, more than just about anyone. It's a different mask to the one I wore outside. That was the coolness mask, trying to look cool, dress cool, say all the right things, never put a foot wrong. That failed me and I ended up in here. Now I have the mask of silence: my cold frozen one, where I don't risk showing anything. It's a kind of non-mask mask. Talking to Esther, two nights ago, talking to Oliver occasionally, they're the only times I've opened up a bit. I don't risk it much with the therapists, even Dr Singh, and I never risk it in Group.

When I think about the other kids, though, I suppose most of them do still keep some sort of mask here. That is, when they're not crying or talking honestly about their lives, their problems. Cindy's mask is to be tough and aggressive sometimes, whiney and pathetic other times. Emine's is to be sweet and kind to everyone. Ben, well, his is pretty obvious, keeping on the move, being stupid, never staying in one place long enough for anyone to get to know him. Oliver, he's sort of polite and reserved: a bit like me, only I'm colder. Daniel, I don't think he has a mask. He just keeps away from anyone he thinks might be cruel to him. Oh wait, yes, I guess he does hide stuff. He usually acts pretty laid-back, making witty jokes about everything, but I know from things he's said in Group that he's not very happy inside.

Guess none of us is happy, no matter how much we pretend, or we wouldn't be here.

Esther, now she really doesn't have a mask. I used to think she was too crazy to bother with one; too crazy to put one together. But now I think it's more that she's a very honest person. From the way she describes her family—the way they used to live—I'd say they just weren't into the fakery that's an everyday thing in my life, my world.

That's what I like most about dogs. They don't wear masks, ever. Checkers never had a mask. What you saw was what you got. When Checkers felt sad his tail drooped, his head drooped, his ears drooped. When he felt guilty he walked past you quite quickly, on his toes, keeping a safe distance and looking at you out of the corners of his eyes. When he was happy, which was most of the time, he sparkled around the house, whooping and yelling with joy, tail out of control.

In Group today, Marj tried to get Emine to say more. I mean to really say something. Emine talks plenty in Group, but it wasn't till Marj started working on her that I realised Emine's comments are always about other people. It's like when the spotlight is focussed on her she grabs it and quickly turns it onto someone else. Marj is pretty smart at times. Emine is school phobic, something I'd never heard of before. When I did have it explained to me, by Oliver actually, I thought it was a joke. I mean, doesn't every kid have school phobia? Oliver didn't think it was a joke, but he never quite succeeded in convincing me.

When Marj put the heat on her today, Emine got pretty upset. At first she sounded as sweet and natural as ever, but gradually her voice dropped and her head went down and her beautiful dark skin got even darker. She said she didn't know why she had been put in hospital, there was nothing wrong with her. Well, we've all said that sometime in here. The stupid thing about psych wards is that one of your symptoms is you think nothing's wrong with you, and that's a very serious symptom. So probably the whole population should be in here, because most people think there's not too much wrong with them. I got that from *Catch-22*.

And the more you complain that you're fine, the longer they're likely to keep you here. Catch-22 again.

For a long time this morning Emine was saying she was happy at school, happy at home, loved her parents, had lots of friends. Then gradually she started being more honest. Seems like her parents wanted to control every aspect of her life. They were so strict and made her dress so conservatively that she felt conspicuous at school. She was embarrassed to talk to other kids because their lives seemed so different. She couldn't ask anyone home because her family lived in such a traditional way that she thought they'd look like freaks . . . even though there were quite a few students from other cultures at her school, and quite a few of them lived in traditional ways at home. But at school they acted like their lives were episodes from an American sitcom.

That was one thing her school had in common with mine.

Emine went to an all-girls' school, same as me, except that hers wasn't a private one. But there was a girl there, Turkish-Australian, same as Emine, who had a brother who'd seen Emine at the bus stop, and he really liked her. I could see why: Emine is one of the most beautiful people I've ever seen, with her long black hair and dark eyes, like chocolate, dark chocolate.

The brother wanted to ring Emine, but Emine knew that wouldn't work, because her parents screened her phone calls and would never allow her to talk to a boy. So they agreed that the other girl would ring up and ask to talk to Emine. She would say they had to discuss some homework. When Emine was given the phone the girl would put her brother on.

It worked the first two times but then it fell apart. Emine was talking to the boy when her father got suspicious. He lifted the extension phone to listen. As soon as Emine heard the click on the line she knew what was happening, but the boy was talking and did not hear it. He continued to talk on happily as Emine stood there trembling. When Emine's father heard the male voice he stormed in and cut off the call. He started hitting Emine around the head as she backed away, screaming. Her mother ran in. When she realised what Emine had done, she was horrified, scandalised, but at least she wouldn't let her husband beat Emine, which was what he wanted to do. But all evening they shouted at her, telling her how she had disgraced them, shamed them.

Emine said the worst thing was that both of them, but especially her mother, assumed that Emine had been meeting the boy, doing awful things with him. They told her she was a slut.

I thought that anyone less like a slut than Emine was hard to imagine.

This was the worst thing because up until then Emine and her mother had got on well, had supported each other when her father was being especially outrageous and unreasonable. Now her mother turned on her and made it clear that she didn't trust her at all.

After that, Emine found it more and more difficult to go to school. She imagined that everyone knew about her disgrace, that they were all talking about her. She was embarrassed to tell her friend that the brother could not call anymore, even though the girl, coming from a similar background, seemed to understand. But to Emine, every other girl at school seemed to have such a free and easy life, able to go down to the shopping centre after school, go out at night, talk freely to boys, even choose their own boyfriends.

"I started getting sick," she whispered. "And I couldn't go to school. It was terrible. I had stomach cramps, I was vomiting, I got these awful headaches." She missed a day or two a week, then three or four days a week, till she was hardly going at all. Gradually the counsellor at school, then doctors and social workers, got involved. Things built up to a point where one night, when the doctor was talking to her, Emine became hysterical. That's the night she ended up in hospital.

For Emine, as for all of us in one way or another, coming in here wasn't the end of our problems. In some ways it was just the start. Emine's parents freaked out. They couldn't cope. They thought it was more shame, more disgrace for the family.

One of the things Emine found hardest in Group was talking about her parents. She felt it was disloyal to criticise them in front of us. She felt it was disloyal to criticise them at all. Even though she was so nice to Cindy, in Group and out of it, she was shocked at the way Cindy spoke about her parents.

I'm a bit like that too. Most of us are, I think. Writing about stuff in here is easier than saying it out loud in Group. It's especially hard when my father's been in the news so much. I don't want to make things any worse for him than they are already. I'm scared that if I say stuff in here it might get out to the papers or on TV or something. I feel that the other kids, and even the staff, are too curious about our family, wanting to know how much of what they read was true. I feel I've done enough damage already.

So I can sympathise with Emine. Funny really, I sympathise with everyone in here, even Cindy.

Everyone except one person.

nine

THE MORE CHECKERS GREW, the funnier his coat looked. The black and white squares got more conspicuous, and because none of them matched up, he looked like a weird moving chess game. People laughed at them, at him, but he didn't mind. He trotted self-importantly down the street, taking no notice of people, intent on the lampposts and garden walls and footpaths. He could have been mistaken for a piece of paving that had escaped from a driveway and gone feral.

Normally I hate to stand out. I don't like being conspicuous. I was conspicuous when I was walking Checkers, but it wasn't the same, because the attention was directed at him, not me. Anyway, I liked him so much that I wouldn't have cared if he looked like the Abominable Snowman.

We got pretty conspicuous when the *Advocate* broke its story, of course. Over the years I'd become used to being envied by some girls. I hadn't noticed it when I was little, but by about Grade 4 I knew what was going on. I'd worked out what counted. You had to have the big house, the right car, the glamorous-looking mum. And by Grade 4, I knew our house and our cars and my mum were good enough.

In those days, even when Rider Group got negative publicity, it never altered the main things. Rider Group was so big, so powerful, that nothing really touched it. But this story was different. It was too big to go away. The papers, TV, radio, they all ran with it. Reporters started calling the house, even turning up at odd times of day looking for a story. Dad and Mum kept warning us not to talk to them—not that we needed much warning. Like I said, we'd been taught from our cradles to be discreet, not to repeat things that we heard from Jack or Dad.

I got into a routine when a reporter came to the house. Mark usually left it to me to answer the bell. I'd open the door and there'd be this smooth-looking man or woman, sometimes with a photographer, sometimes not.

"Yes?" I'd go.

"Uh, is Mr Warner home?"

"No, he's not."

"Do you know what time he'll be back?"

"Yes, but he doesn't give interviews at home. You'll have to call his office."

"Are you his daughter?"

"Sorry, I'm not allowed to talk to you guys."

"Well, could I just ask you . . ."

"Sorry, I think the washing machine's flooding again." And I'd close the door.

As time went on, my excuses for shutting the door got more and more bizarre, till Mark used to listen from the dining room, his hand over his mouth to stop himself laughing. "Sorry, I think the oven's just exploded . . . Sorry, I'm missing *Wheel of Fortune* . . . my baby needs its nappies changed . . . my brother'll escape if I don't get in there and tie him up properly . . ."

I didn't make those jokes when TV cameras were there, of course. I didn't want to see myself on the evening news saying dumb things. But it was nice to be able to shut the door in people's faces and not get in trouble for it.

There was a lull for a few days after the *Advocate*'s triple-header story, when they didn't seem to come up with anything new. I thought the whole thing would die a natural death, which is what Dad always said would happen. No such luck. The next shock came about a week later, when the TV show *Day's End* fired a whole new blast. It was the lead story, at six o'clock, and they'd been advertising it all afternoon, so we knew it was coming. Mark and I were the only ones home. Mark stood in the doorway watching, but kind of half-hidden behind the door. I lounged in the big red armchair with Checkers's head on my lap. I was scratching his ear as I started watching, but I soon stopped doing that and concentrated on the screen.

It was pretty bad. Somehow, probably illegally, they'd got hold of telephone records from Mr Koneckny's private number. They'd found eight overseas phone calls to American hotels and, by a strange coincidence, they were the same hotels where members of the Casino Commission were staying on their tour of overseas casinos. The dates matched exactly. Most of the conversations were around five to ten minutes, but the longest was an hour and a half.

As if that wasn't enough, they'd traced a whole lot of payments, that they said were secret, from Rider Group to overseas. One of them was to a company in the Bahamas, but at least it wasn't the one that bought the shares. None of the companies looked too good, though. They were all funny shadowy little ones in overseas countries, companies that had untraceable directors and paid-up capitals of anything from two dollars to a thousand. Not good. The payments came to about four and a half million dollars in eight months and, according to *Day's End,* they didn't show up in Rider Group accounts.

The Opposition, with Mrs O'Shea in full flight, was calling for a Royal Commission. Mrs O'Shea said the scandal had now come right into the Premier's office and the only way for people to be satisfied was to have a full inquiry. It was the first time I'd heard it called a scandal. The Deputy Chairman was under huge pressure, because he'd issued a statement after the *Advocate* story to say they'd only had a few, official, contacts with Mr Koneckny.

The one piece of good news so far was that there was no connection between the Premier, Koneckny, the Commission, and Dad and Jack. Mark and I knew there must be a connection, because how else would we have known we'd got the contract way back in March? The secret was safe with us, but how many other people were in the know?

As soon as the story ended, Mark disappeared to his bedroom. I had no-one I could talk to. I went to bed early and slept badly.

Next morning on the radio came the news of the first victim. Or sacrifice, as some people called him. The Premier announced that Mr Koneckny had been sacked for misleading him. He said Mr Koneckny had had contacts with the Commission on his own initiative, without telling the Premier. His motives were good but he couldn't be allowed to have his own agenda, and so he had reluctantly asked for Mr Koneckny's resignation. I stayed home, partly because I couldn't face school, partly because I wanted to see what else would happen. By lunchtime the Commission's Deputy Chairman had resigned, denying wrongdoing but admitting that he had "forgotten" some "inconsequential" chats with Mr Koneckny.

By three o'clock Jack had issued a statement that any conversations between Koneckny and anyone else were none of Rider Group's business, and it shouldn't get in the way of their job, which was to build and operate the casino. At 3:25 P.M. the Premier was interviewed on the *George Polaris Show*: he said that nothing had changed. The best tender had won the contract and no review was needed.

On the evening news Dad was interviewed. He said that Rider Group had done nothing improper with its transfers of money around the world. It was normal business practice, but the details had to remain confidential.

They couldn't let their competitors know everything they were doing.

Dad looked tired and irritated. To my surprise he walked in the door about five minutes after the interview ended. He looked even worse than he had on TV.

"I just saw you," I said.

"Saw me? Oh, you mean on TV. They taped that this afternoon." He sorted through the mail. "So, how'd I look?"

"Tired."

"Oh well. That figures. How'd I sound?"

"Convincing."

"Good."

"It's a bit of a mess, isn't it?"

"Typical business problems. We're not worried. We've been through worse."

"No you haven't," I thought. Out loud, I said, "There've been more reporters calling. I took a few messages. They're on the pad at the hall phone."

"OK, thanks honey," he said, but I don't think he'd really heard me.

He went through to the kitchen and I followed, watching as he started to make a sandwich. "What's in the fridge?" he asked, as he spread the bread.

I opened the door and reported. "Couple of slices of ham, turning up at the edges. Half a tomato. Bit of lettuce. Lots of cheese. Pâté, but I don't like the colour of it."

"OK, I'll have the tomato, and you pick me a cheese that looks interesting."

"So are you going to get out of all this?" I asked, as I sliced some cheese for him.

He shrugged. “Sure. It’ll blow over.”

“But it’s getting so serious, with the Premier and everything.”

He was about to take his first bite of sandwich, but he stopped and looked down at a stain on the table.

“That’s the biggest thing,” he said, almost to himself, then to me he said: “We’ll be OK as long as there’s no connection between us and the Premier. Koneckny, he’s an idiot. He nearly screwed the whole thing up. I warned Jack, but he wouldn’t listen. But I think the damage can be stopped now. The Premier’s big enough and powerful enough to do anything at the moment.” He shook his head, almost in admiration, and took the first bite. “He’s amazing,” he said, through the sandwich, smiling at me. “He just does what he wants. No-one’s strong enough to stand up to him. The press, the Opposition, least of all his own party. They’re pretty pathetic really.”

My father always seemed to have too much respect for strong people, people like Jack.

“Do you know him?” I asked, trying to look cool, but holding my breath as I waited for the answer.

“The Premier? No, never met him before in my life.”

I knew he was lying. Or else why’d he say “before”?

ten

Daniel got really twitchy in Group today and Marj noticed, as she notices everything. Group can be a kind of game sometimes, when someone decides she wants a bit of attention. It's usually Cindy. She sits there looking so sad and depressed, head down, ignoring people when they try to talk to her, till Marj finally says, "I think we have one person in Group today who's feeling particularly upset," and we all look at Cindy and make sympathetic noises and wait for her to spill her guts.

When Marj is away, as she is often, like every second day—I don't know how she has the cheek to collect her pay some weeks—her replacement, Lesley, is almost exactly the same but not quite. It's like a cardboard cutout of Marj, or a Marj doll, because the words are the same but they come out of Lesley's mouth at a slightly different speed, and she says some words differently.

Anyway today it was Marj and, instead of Cindy being the drama queen, it was Daniel. Whoops, I didn't mean that the way it sounded. Even if Daniel would have been the first to laugh.

He wouldn't have laughed today, though. He wasn't in laughter mode. He wouldn't say anything for quite a while, but finally, with Marj prodding away, he whispered, "I feel awful."

"I think it's something to do with Noel," Cindy said.

"Noel the patient in F11?"

"Mmm."

Noel's one of the adult patients. I've never been quite sure what I think about him. He's fat and jolly, cheerful with the other adults and impossible to beat at table tennis. He's got the most vicious serve I've ever seen, and for a big guy he's quick on his feet. But with us kids he's a bit, I don't know, there's something a bit nasty about him. He hangs around us quite a lot, and I think he feels we should look up to him, treat him with respect. He gets a little pissed off when we laugh at him. So all the jolliness stuff—sometimes I wonder if it's just a front.

Daniel still wouldn't say anything, so Cindy told her story. "Last night I saw Daniel sitting outside having a durry and I thought I'd have one too, so I went to get some money from my room for the cigarette machine. Noel was just coming past and he asked me for a smoke but I said I didn't have any, which was true. He went outside and I went down to the machine. When I got outside Daniel asked me for a cigarette and I gave him one, then Noel asked me for one again, but he's always bolting smokes, so I wouldn't give him one. Then I went inside to get a jumper, because it was so cold last night, and when I came out again I couldn't find Daniel. I couldn't figure it out, because he'd been there two minutes earlier, about to light his smoke, and now he was gone. So I went up to his room to look for him, but he wasn't there either: like, the room was empty. But just as I was going out I thought I heard a noise from the cupboard, so I opened it and there was Daniel, all scrunched up and crying. I got such a shock, because the cupboard wouldn't be the cleanest place in the world and you know what Daniel's like about dirt. Anyway, he wouldn't tell me what was wrong but after a while he asked me to take him down to the boys' bathroom. And on the way there he said if we saw Noel not to stop, just keep walking. Well, we didn't see him, but that's why I think it had something to do with Noel."

"You had a long shower last night, Daniel," Ben said.

Lately Daniel's cut his shower times down to only an hour a day, most days, so a long one was bad news. I figured Marj would know all about that, though. The staff know everything that happens, everything we do. It's enough to make you paranoid, which means you'd stay here forever then. Catch-22.

So Marj started in on Daniel. She might have already known what upset him anyway, because if the night staff knew, they'd have put it down in the case notes and talked about it when they had their little change-of-shifts ceremony. If you asked for a smaller helping of apple pie at teatime that was a symptom of something and they wrote it down.

"Daniel, you seem to have had a bad night?"

No response.

"Have you talked to anyone about it?"

No response.

"Did something specific happen to upset you?"

Long, long pause, then a tiny nod.

"Something last night?"

Ditto long pause, tiny nod.

"Is Cindy right about Noel being involved?"

Daniel didn't respond to that at all, so Marj tried again.

In Marj's book, any reaction is a good reaction. They don't care if you cry, scream, yell with rage, attack them—verbally, anyway. The only thing they can't stand is what I give them. Silence. Passivity. Nothing.

So she must have been pleased with what she suddenly got from Daniel. He burst into a flood of tears, crying noisily, rocking himself backwards and forwards. I moved over and put my arm around him. I hate seeing anyone unhappy. But it was about five minutes before he calmed down.

"How're you feeling, Daniel?" Marj asked.

That's their standard question. I wish I had a gold medal for every time I heard it. My trophy cabinet would be full. You'd think it'd be obvious how Daniel was feeling. He was gulping and sobbing but he finally managed to say, "Awful."

We were all sitting there, pretty tense. No matter how often you see someone crack up, it's powerful. We all like Daniel, I think, even Ben, who's so nervous of him. And although Daniel is an emotional guy, kind of brittle, and he does give the impression that he's covering up and could easily snap, I'd never seen him like this.

"Do you feel you can talk about it?" Marj asked.

"He . . . he called me a fairy," Daniel hiccuped.

"A fairy?"

"Yeah, a fairy, a poofter, all those names, you know. When Cindy wouldn't give him a cigarette."

"But you make jokes like that yourself," Oliver said, looking slightly surprised.

"But it's different then," Daniel said. "I do it to stop other people doing it."

"How do you mean?"

"Well, I sort of beat them to it," Daniel explained. "If I do it, they don't bother. Or if they do, it doesn't matter so much."

I understood what he meant then. It was a smart tactic.

"So you do mind all that stuff," Oliver said.

"Of course I mind," Daniel said. He sat up a bit. He was still crying but he was getting angry too. "Of course I mind. You think I like it? I can't help the way I am. I didn't choose to be this way. But this is the way I am, this is me, I just want people to accept it. But some of the kids at school, even people in my own family, and now people here, they can't leave me alone."

"No-one in this group gives you a hard time," Oliver said.

"Some of you do."

There was silence for a bit.

"What are your parents like?" Cindy asked.

"They're OK. They're cool. They just tell me to be

myself, not to worry what people say. But that doesn't help much."

"How can you not worry what people say?" Emine asked.

"I can't," Daniel said miserably. "I just think this is going to keep happening all my life."

"Do you like the way you are?" Cindy asked. She was being pretty good today, like she really cared.

Daniel considered. "I don't know. Sometimes. I think I've got some good points."

"Such as?" Marj said.

"I try to be nice to people," Daniel said. "I work pretty hard. I try to do the right things, most of the time."

"What do you want to be when you leave school?" Cindy asked.

"I used to think I'd like to be a social worker," Daniel said. "But I don't know, I doubt if they'd take me after being in here."

"Why not?" Emine asked.

"Well you know, being in a psych hospital, it's not exactly the perfect background for it, is it? They'd think I'd crack up under pressure."

I couldn't help myself, I had to say something. It was too awful to see Daniel so miserable, tearing himself apart. So I spoke.

"I think you'd be a good social worker, after being in here," I whispered.

Marj just about slid off her chair. But she was too well trained for that. She got red in the face and sat up a bit.

"Sorry, didn't quite catch that," she said. "Would you mind repeating it?"

So I did. What the hell, it was about time. But I could understand her getting excited. They were the first words I'd ever spoken in Group.

eleven

DANIEL BEING SO UPSET made me think. Everyone's problems are different, but they're the same in a lot of ways. One thing about all of us is that we don't have any skin. People talk about thick skin and thin skin, but we don't have any, or we wouldn't be in here. When people like Noel attack us, we've got no way of holding them off.

It's bad enough with Noel, who's not much more than a stranger. It's a lot worse when it's someone close, like your own family for instance.

I was never thick-skinned, but I was better than I am now. Somehow I've lost whatever skin I had.

When things started going wrong with Dad and Rider Group it was bad, but it was still bearable. I almost got used to the front-page stories, the current affairs shows on TV. You could tell that most days they didn't have anything new. I didn't read many of the stories in the paper, and I got into the habit of taking Checkers for a walk when the current affairs shows came on at six-thirty. The worst part was that Dad and Mum and Mark, and yes, me too, stopped functioning as a family. Once Mum got over the first shock she became kind of housebound. She scrubbed harder, polished harder, cleaned more, but she hardly ever went anywhere. Dad couldn't understand that, and it made him mad, but he didn't seem able to do much about it. I couldn't understand it myself, and it made me mad too.

It was about eight o'clock on a Tuesday night when we reached the next stage of awfulness. A reporter had been hanging around for nearly two hours. He rang the bell and asked to talk to Dad.

"He's not home yet."

"Can I ask when you're expecting him?"

"I don't know. Probably quite late. But I don't think he'll give you an interview here."

I was getting more polite to them, I suppose because I had some vague idea that they'd be kinder to us. I guess that was a bit naive.

I shut the door and the man wandered back to the street. I watched him through the window. He had a conference with his photographer, and they settled down on the front wall to wait. I didn't look at them again. We were so used to them by now. I even knew this one's name: Allan Watkins, from the *Standard.*

When Dad finally drove in I was sitting at my desk, trying to do homework. I got up to put some hot water on, in case he wanted a coffee. On the way to the kitchen I heard loud voices, angry voices, from outside, and I stopped and looked through the window. There was Dad, yelling at the reporter. He was waving his arms around like an AFL goal umpire with his flags. The reporter was only a metre from him, standing with his arms folded, not moving. The photographer was about five metres to Dad's right, out of his line of vision, snapping away non-stop, having a great time. I paused, not knowing what to do. If I went outside I might make things worse. If I stayed inside things might get worse anyway. Mum was home, but having a sleep in her bedroom. She slept a lot these days. Mark was out. There was no-one to tell me what to do. After a minute, as the voices got louder and Dad's arms even more violent, I thought I'd better go out there. Dad looked like he might hit someone at any moment. I went to the front door, pulled it open and went out. And just as I stepped onto the lawn it all exploded.

Dad pulled back his right arm and hit the reporter somewhere round the middle of his face. The reporter grabbed his nose and buckled at the knees. As he dropped, Dad pushed him backwards, so that he lost balance completely. The photographer didn't do a thing to help his mate, just kept taking photos. Mr Watkins was lying on his back on the grass, holding his nose and moaning. I ran towards them, praying like mad that he wasn't hurt. Not that I cared about him; I just didn't want Dad to get in more trouble. But then I saw blood on Mr Watkins's face. Dad was standing over him, not saying anything, just looking grim. For a moment the only sound was the "scarritch, scarritch" of the camera.

Then Mr Watkins yelled up at him, "You stupid bastard, what did you do that for?"

I reached Dad at that moment and grabbed him. I was scared he'd hit the reporter again. But he let me pull him away so Mr Watkins could get up. He got out a handkerchief and held it to his nose to soak up the blood. No-one said anything. They just stood there glaring at each other. The photographer was changing film cartridges, I think. I was the first to speak.

"Are you all right?" I asked Mr Watkins.

"No, I'm not," he said, answering me but looking straight at Dad.

"Do you want to come in the house?" I asked. "To clean up?"

"No," he said. Then he turned to the photographer. "Let's get out of here," he said.

Even Dad could tell by the tone of his voice that the situation was desperate. Dad put out a hand to stop him. "Look," he said, "I'm sorry. I lost my head. I didn't mean to hurt you. Come inside and clean up, and have a drink. You too," he said to the photographer.

But they ignored him. The photographer picked up his bag and the reporter looked around for his notebook. I saw it, and his pen, a few metres away, so I picked them up and handed them to him. He didn't thank me, just walked away, he and the photographer, to their car, which was parked outside the Sykeses'.

Dad stood there without moving. His head was down. I felt sorry for him, but I felt sort of masterful, in control. "Come on," I said. "You'd better have that drink yourself."

He followed me into the house and I got him a whisky. He sat there for about two hours, not saying anything. I tried a few times to get him to talk, but he wouldn't. I cooked him some tea but he wasn't interested.

Eventually Mum came out of their bedroom. She looked at us and seemed to realise something was wrong. "What's happened?" she asked. He took her back into their room and shut the door. I could hear them talking for hours.

When Mark got home—he'd been to Josh's—I told him about it. But he didn't seem to react—just listened to what I said, then disappeared to his own room. In the end, I gave up and went to bed.

Next morning I dreaded to look at the *Standard.* But I thought I'd better so I'd know what to expect at school.

"It couldn't be worse," was my first thought. In fact, the time came when I realised things could always be worse. But I didn't quite realise that then. I stared at the page in horror, not knowing whether to read the story or look at the pictures. It was all over the front page, of course, but there was heaps more inside. Photos of Dad throwing the punch, of the punch connecting, of the push, of the reporter lying on the ground. It said he had to go to hospital to have his nose X-rayed, and that he was considering legal action against Dad. I don't suppose that surprised me.

But what worried me as much as all that was the story behind the punch; the story of what he had said that made Dad lose his temper. It turned out there was more trouble about the contract. The paper said that one of the other bidders, a company I'd never heard of called Jackson Investments, had bid fifteen million dollars more than Rider Group. No-one would confirm it—there was a series of "no comments" from all the people involved—but the paper swore its information was from "a reliable source." The main editorial said that there'd have to be an inquiry, a Royal Commission preferably.

By itself it was no worse than all the other stories. It was just the sense that this was never going to go away; that it was going to keep getting worse and worse and worse. The Premier was famous for taking no notice of the press: it was his proud boast that "I run this state, and the newspapers don't." In the last election the Opposition had run an ad showing the Premier with a bubble coming out of his mouth saying, "I am the Premier. Shut up."

But even he couldn't ignore this much longer. It was stinking worse than the Cheshunt Abattoirs. I was keeping my eyes closed and my nose firmly pegged, but the smell was starting to seep into me too.

twelve

Oh, such a long day, such a hard one. Ever since the time I spoke in Group, told Daniel he'd make a good social worker, Marj has been putting pressure on me. Dr Singh too. I think they're hoping I'll be their star patient, the psych legend, make them famous at conferences from here to the Gold Coast. But I haven't done as they hoped: I haven't said much else in Group.

No, today was hard because of Cindy. She's been in trouble for a long time. She keeps fighting the staff, abusing them, not doing what they want. For instance, we're meant to write heaps of stuff, as part of our programme. Sometimes I think I do more writing in here than I ever did at school. We have to write about our family, like who's the boss and what they do to hold that position (make that who *was* the boss in my family), who's the most submissive (used to be Mark, really, even more than Mum, which did surprise me when I realised that—score one to you, Dr Singh), what things caused the most arguments. Even though my family's changed so much, I still have to do it. But Cindy's either too lazy or too something, I don't know what. She never does any, and no matter how much pressure they put on her, it makes no difference.

Her parents came to visit a few times lately, not just for Family Therapy but for real visits, but it didn't seem to help. They always looked so pale and grim, as though Cindy being in here was the end of the world. Matter of fact, most of the parents who visit look like that. Especially when their kids are being admitted. You see them down in Reception, and it's like "Ohmygod, how could this happen to us? Where did we go wrong? What will I tell my friends at tennis on Tuesday?"

Cindy was always hopeless when her parents came, ratty at everyone, foul to them. She reminded me of a feral cat I once saw being pulled out of a trap by Peter the Possum Man. Spitting and kicking and yowling: that was Cindy. Her parents looked all right to me, but I mean, how can you tell? They all know how to look, especially in the kind of suburbs we live in.

One of the complications was that even in here Cindy lived a double life. There was the way she was around the staff and the way she was with us. Most patients give up on that kind of game when they come in here. We don't have the energy for it anymore. But Cindy kept it going. For instance, she has this friend who works in the pub around the corner, and a couple of times she's talked the staff into letting her go to the milk bar for an ice cream or a Mars bar. That's what she says she's doing. What she really does is go straight to her mate in the pub and pick up a bottle of something toxic. Last week it was a litre of vodka. We mixed it with Fanta. By lunchtime the bottle was empty. We were kind of rowdy all afternoon. I don't know if Marj noticed anything, but I guess we got away with it. Yesterday it was half a dozen cans of UDL, the vodka and orange, I think. I didn't get to see it. I didn't get an invitation. For once I got lucky, because they were busted when Daniel was sick in the corridor, right near the nurses' station. He tried to make it to the bathroom and failed. Big mess on the carpet, and bigger mess for Cindy, when they found out she'd brought it in.

They were really angry. Sometimes, just when you've decided they're all friendly and nice in here, they pull some totally fascist act, like turning off the TV five minutes from the end of a movie and making us go to bed. The way they went after Cindy, it was like we were back at school. They called her parents in and did the whole number. Fair enough, I suppose, but it freaked me out a bit. These days I can't handle conflict at all, any kind of conflict. If I see someone arguing with the kitchen lady about the ice cream being too soft, I'm like, "Beam me out of here."

So Cindy got it from everyone: Dr Singh, Marj, Sister Allen, even the night staff. No-one could have predicted what she'd do. She came to Group this morning but she wouldn't say anything, even though Marj wanted to talk about it. Daniel, Oliver, Ben and even Emine owned up to drinking, so in the end Marj just concentrated on them and explained how dangerous alcohol was with our treatment and medication and stuff. Then sometime before lunch they found Cindy hacking away at her wrist with a pair of scissors she'd pinched from the nurses' station. Luckily they got to her before she'd done much damage. They dressed her wrist and bandaged it. And then they committed her.

It was horrible. We're all voluntary patients here, so anyone who's committed gets taken off to Janda Park. I've only seen it once before, with an old guy who started attacking the orderlies because he said they were agents of the devil.

An ambulance came at about five o'clock, with two policemen. Apparently you've got to have cops when someone's committed. It's the law. It was the same when they took the old guy, but I thought it'd be different for Cindy, seeing she's young and not dangerous or anything. Cindy looked absolutely terrified. Why wouldn't she? She stood there, so pale-faced and thin, between these two big cops. We all said goodbye. She just smiled at us and said, "Don't worry, I'll be fine," and stuff like that, but you could see how scared she was. It was as though the spirit had gone out of her.

I feel bad now that I was so bitchy to her. I didn't like her before but when I saw her standing there behind the ambulance, suddenly I felt I really liked her. Bit late for that. But that's me all over, changing my mind too late.

I feel lonely tonight. I miss my family, even if they are such a mess. I even miss Mark. I can't bring myself to think about what's happened, what I did. I don't know, I suppose all the stuff leading up to the big disaster wasn't my fault. It just took me to finish it off. I can't stop thinking about it. Without me it might still have worked out OK. When Dad punched out the reporter, that was bad. Maybe that was the beginning of the end. It encouraged all the other reporters to start hounding him more and more. They thought it proved that he was a weak link, that they might get more good footage if they pushed him enough. If he'd taken out a gun and shot one of them, the others would have been totally rapt. It would have given them such a great story.

What happened, though, was that things went quiet again for a while. Mr Watkins sued for assault, and Dad was summonsed for it as well. He settled the civil case out of court, straightaway, and the criminal case got adjourned for four months. He had enough self-control not to hit anyone else. He was very quiet at home, hardly spoke to anyone, and when he did it was only a word or two: "No," "Yes," "Pass the salt, please, Mark," "Get that dog away from the table."

To Dad Checkers was always "that dog."

The only new story that the papers played around with was a rumour that Dad had had a secret meeting with the Premier in March. The Premier issued another statement denying he'd ever met Dad. But the big issue was still the contacts between Mr Koneckny and the Deputy Chairman of the Commission. Although they'd both been chucked out of their jobs, the press was screaming for an explanation of what their conversations were about. They both said it was just general chitchat about the inquiry, nothing sinister or illegal. The Premier said he believed them and wasn't going to waste public money on a Royal Commission. And it seemed to rest there. No-one had anything new and the Premier seemed like he was going to ride out the storm, as he'd done plenty of times before. The opinion polls had him eight points ahead, so I guess he wasn't too worried.

One night Dad announced we were going skiing. He took me by surprise. He hadn't done anything spontaneous for months, apart from punching out the reporter. There was still a week of school to go but that didn't bother him: there'd been a good dump, the best of the year, and he wanted to go tomorrow, tonight, this instant.

We went the next day. The worst thing was putting Checkers into kennels. I felt like I'd abandoned him when I saw his sad face peering through the wire netting of his pen and heard his yelping begin as I walked away. Poor thing, he'd never been left before. The lady who owned the kennels made it worse by laughing at Checkers when she saw him. "Goodness, he's an unusual one," she said. "Where'd you get him?"

I'd never actually asked Dad where he got Checkers. He'd said something about a friend who'd been looking for a home for a dog, that was all. In the car on the way back from the kennels I asked him some more. I was always kind of nervous when I was alone with Dad, so it was good to have a topic to talk about for once; a safe topic.

"Oh, I got him from a business friend," he said vaguely, as he tried to sneak through a gap in the traffic at a roundabout. "No-one you've met."

"How many puppies were in the litter?"

"Just the two. The mother wasn't meant to breed with the father. She's a pedigree cocker spaniel, he's a crossbreed Border collie from down the road. Your dog's lucky he wasn't drowned at birth."

"What happened to the other one?"

"They kept him, I think. His wife, I think she wanted to have him. She was the one who stopped them being drowned in the first place."

"Does Checkers look like his brother?"

"Yes, very, as I recall. I didn't take a lot of notice. It all happened kind of quickly, on the spur of the moment. I was so excited about . . . there was so much happening that day . . . well, my mind was on other things, put it that way."

The next morning we left for Mt Whiteman. That's always been my favourite, that and Tremblant, when we've been to Canada a few times. Whiteman's a long drive, and I get carsick going up the last bit, but it's a small price to pay. We stopped at Bronson for lunch and to hire some chains (Dad hadn't got around to buying new ones since we changed cars) and I bought some very cool, very expensive Ray Bans. Everyone seemed more relaxed, happier; even Mum. She doesn't like skiing, and we'd had to work hard to persuade her to come, but I was glad we had when I saw her going through the clothes racks in the ski shop, just like old times.

The weather was pretty foul but we got to the carpark without using the chains and caught a Toyota up to the hotel. We were staying in The Max, a new place, very big, a bit over the top with all the white marble and chandeliers, but at least the rooms weren't pokey like they are in a lot of ski lodges. Mark and I had to share a room because the place was so heavily booked, but even though he dropped his stuff all over the floor as per usual, I could still get from the bed to the door and back without breaking a leg.

I saw Susy Thieu the moment I arrived. I assumed she'd given school the flick for a few days, same as me, but it turned out she was with the PLC ski team, training for the inter-schools. Within three minutes she introduced me to six guys, so I was set. I knew I wouldn't be seeing much of Mummy and Daddy, let alone little brother, for the next week.

I've got a theory about skiing, and that is that you improve over the summer without having to do anything. In other words, whatever standard you're at when one season ends, you start the next season at a higher standard. It's not very logical, but I honestly believe it works that way. So I felt good the next morning. I'd had the skis tuned and waxed and whatever else they do to them, the snow was good, I'd been on 195s for half of last season and was confident, so I just went for it. The weather was lousy: windy and cold, with bad visibility, little ice particles blowing straight into our faces. Hardly anyone was around. Mark came with me but Mum and Dad were still in bed.

For three hours we skied our asses off. Mark's better than me, technically, but I'm more aggressive, and that morning he really had to struggle to keep up. "Suck on it, little brother," I thought, skiing straight onto yet another lift without him.

"What's the hurry?" he asked me at one point. "It'll still be here tomorrow, you know."

I didn't know what the hurry was. I still don't. I wasn't thinking about it. I just wanted to go as far and as fast as I could. I flashed past people at Concorde speed, not caring if I ran them off the slopes or into trees. I made my knees work like they were on springs. I skied every slope on the mountain, and invented a few runs of my own. "You're crazy," Mark said as he caught up with me in the lift queue, still huffing and puffing from a great route I'd just found, down the side of McCaskills Shoulder.

He was right, of course, and my being in here proves it. Except I more or less know why I'm in here. I don't know why I was crazy that day. But suddenly it was over. Suddenly I felt the numb coldness of my face, the burning red skin, the sandblasted cheeks. I felt the ache of my knees. I felt the rumbles of ravenous hunger in my stomach. I turned to Mark.

"I'm going back," I said.

"I thought you'd never ask," he grumbled.

I wasn't actually asking, just telling, but I think he was too wrecked to know the difference.

The rest of the six days was totally different to that first morning. I hung round with Susy and the PLC squad, stole their guys off them—well, tried to—gave my fake ID a huge workout, partied, skied, and partied some more. You don't have time to get tired because everything just keeps happening around you and all you've gotta do is hang on to the roller coaster and not think about how tired you are and how long it is since you last had a sleep.

Somewhere in the world right now, I guess, people are skiing and drinking and partying and cracking on to each other but in here our one pathetic attempt has ended with Cindy stabbing her wrist till she's got bloody gashes all over it and then being taken off in an ambulance to a closed ward.

thirteen

I WAS TELLING OLIVER all about our skiing holiday and he sat looking at me with his brown calf eyes and a little smile on his face. When I finished he said, "God, if Marj could hear you now."

"What do you mean?" I asked, although I knew.

"I haven't heard you talk that much since . . . well, I've never heard you talk that much."

"I don't want to end up like Cindy," I said.

It's sad when you look at Oliver and his beautiful big eyes and you realise how beautiful he must have been before he got anorexia. I know looks aren't everything, and I'd rather have a guy with personality than looks any day, but it'd be such a bonus to have both. I remember reading an article in a magazine about what it's like to go out with a stunning-looking guy, and all these girls who'd done it were saying how it's good but sometimes they're up themselves or other girls try to take them off you or no-one notices you anymore. One girl said the guy could never walk past a mirror without stopping to look at himself. Another one said a girl came up to her and whispered, “How could you ever catch a guy as gorgeous as that?” which must have been nice for her self-esteem.

Still, I wouldn’t mind giving it a go. I think I could handle the pressure.

Anyway, Oliver said to me, “So what did go wrong with your family? It all sounds perfect to me.”

“Perfect? You’ve got to be kidding.”

“So what went wrong?”

“Are you serious? Do you really not know?”

“Why should I know? You never say anything in Group, and even when we talk by ourselves, it’s like there’s a whole big area that you avoid.”

“But you must have seen it in the newspapers.”

“Oh sure. But I don’t remember much about it. I didn’t know I was going to meet you one day, so I didn’t take a lot of notice. It was one of those big financial scams, wasn’t it?”

“Thanks a lot.”

I don’t know why I said that. I hadn’t minded him saying it was a scam, not really. After all, that’s what it was, and now everyone knows it. I think I just said it to make him feel guilty. It’s so easy to make Oliver feel guilty. It’s almost a game.

“Oh sorry, sorry.”

“Don’t worry about it.”

He didn’t say anything for a while, which made me feel guilty then. Maybe that was his game, I don’t know.

We just sat there, smoking.

"Well, anyway," he said at last, "I don't know much about it, that's all I was trying to say."

"But Scranton resigned."

"Oh, yes, I remember. That was because of all that stuff, was it?"

I was amazed. This had been a part of my life for so long that I couldn't believe there were people out there who hardly noticed it. People who only read the sports section of the paper, only look at the evening news to see the horror and murder stories; people who yawn anytime you mention politics or business. Oliver's an intelligent guy: it just happens that he's not interested in that stuff. He and millions like him. Maybe all the fears I had, that the staff and patients in here were too interested in me, kind of spying on me, were just my imagination.

It reminded me also of something I used to wonder about a lot. It's like that song in *Camelot,* the musical we put on at school: "What do the simple folk do?" I used to wonder what it was like for people living ordinary lives, where their parents worked in offices and factories and stuff, and they washed the car every Saturday morning, and going to, like, Sizzler's was the biggest thrill of their week. As far as I know none of my friends ever wondered about this stuff, which is another reason I think I'm a bit of a freak, like I don't belong. But I was fascinated by it. What do the other people do? How do they talk to each other? Why do they watch those terrible shows on TV, like *Bloopers* and *Make-a-Date*? I mean, do they really like them? How can they care so much about some stupid football team that they go along dressed in special jumpers and scarves to watch them *train,* for Chrissakes? I mean to watch them *train!* And hanging around shopping centres all the time, after school and weekends even, I mean what's that *like?* Being totally rapt in the fact that your boyfriend's got some revved-up, purple, chrome-gleaming, fat-tyred, over-painted panel van. Maybe I really am a snob, but it's not that exactly. I mean, they have as little understanding of us as I have of them. I just want to try to get a grip on it.

Maybe I will when I get out of here.

Oliver's not that much different to me, really. I mean, not in his background. Sure he lives out in Spicers Gap, but he goes to a private school, Risden, and his father's an advertising executive. His real father I mean: his current stepfather owns a McDonald's, the one before that ran a trucking company, and the one before that had a meat-processing company. Four fathers. Oliver's had so many changes of name that now he doesn't have a surname. He decided about six months ago that he would just be known as Oliver, nothing else. He's the only person I've ever met who doesn't have a surname. He's even made the hospital take his stepfather's name off his files, so now they just have Oliver on them.

He's strong in so many ways, like that, with his name. People who don't know him well, for example Cindy, think he's weak, but that's not the whole story. I suppose you'd have to say it takes a lot of strength not to eat. I don't think that's a weak thing to do. Especially for a boy. I'd never heard of a boy with anorexia till I came in here, but Marj says it's quite common. Oliver doesn't look too bad at the moment, and he is eating three meals a day, but there were times when he was shocking: they wouldn't let him out of bed for a week at one stage, just after he got admitted.

And the way he kept going after me this morning, that was pretty strong. "So what did go wrong with your family?" he asked again.

"What went wrong with yours?" I asked back, trying to throw him off the scent.

He laughed. "Marj would call that a very red herring, a scarlet one. You know what's wrong with mine. I talk about it in Group, you don't."

I was getting scared, like I was going to spill my guts, and I didn't want to. But I did want to, too.

We were already late for Group, so we ground out our smokes, left two more butts on the pile of disgusting dirty old ones already there and went. For once—the only time ever in history—Marj was late too. She arrived at the door at the same time as us.

I don't know what it is about Marj. She sniffs things out better than Checkers, and he was pretty good. He once flushed a rabbit out of a bush at Clifford College, just by smell. He hung around this bush for ages, making little excited whiffling noises, twitching his nose so hard I thought it'd fall off. "Checkers, come here," I kept yelling, but he wouldn't come away, which was unusual for him. He wasn't the world's most obedient dog, but if you got really mad at him he'd generally make a bit of an effort to veer in your direction. Anyway, after about five minutes this rabbit suddenly came belting out of the bush at maximum revs, and the chase was on. Checkers had his ears back, he was flat to the ground and he was focussed. He chased that bunny all around Clifford College. It was funny and embarrassing at the same time. It was a Saturday and they had cricket matches on everywhere but Checkers stopped every game. It wasn't just that he and the rabbit ran through the middle of each one, it was the fact that all the players were pissing themselves laughing so much that no-one could bowl a ball or hold a bat.

Soon the rabbit got so tired that it looked like the end of his bunny days, like he was off to bunny heaven. A few boys tried to help Checkers by making a dive for the rabbit, but he had a neat sidestep. That had already saved him a couple of times because whenever Checkers got too hot on his heels the rabbit would swerve and go in a new direction, and it took Checkers about ten metres to change course. So each time the rabbit would get a break on him again.

Things were looking terminally bad for the rabbit, though. He was slowing right down, running out of puff. But just when Checkers was about to close on him, just when Checkers was opening his jaws for the big one, just as mothers were telling their kids to cover their eyes, the rabbit dived under the Science Block. At Clifford the Science Block is about two centimetres above the ground—well, say ten centimetres—and somehow the rabbit squeezed in there. Checkers had no hope. He'd been cruelly robbed, right at the moment when he thought he had it. He pulled up hard—he had to, or he'd have head-planted into the Science Block—and pranced around barking and yelping and sniffing. "That's the way life is, Checkers," I told him, as I dragged him away.

Next weekend when I went there again to watch the second half of the game (it was Mark's team playing), they had a new sign up: ALL DOGS MUST BE KEPT ON LEASHES. It didn't say anything about rabbits.

But I was very impressed by Checkers's nose. It's not every dog that could have sniffed out a rabbit right in the middle of the city like that.

Well, I guess I'm even writing red herrings now, in here. So, back to today's Group.

OK, we got in there, we had a little discussion about Marj being late, and about Oliver and I being late. We're all meant to have very powerful feelings about anything Marj does, like when she's away, like she so often is, or when she's late, like she never is. But this time we at least got through that fairly quickly. Then, to my horror, she turned to me.

"I think you've been quiet in Group long enough," she said. "I think perhaps it's time you used the Group to help explore some of the reasons you're in hospital."

I was shocked, embarrassed, confused. She wasn't normally assertive like this. She put pressure on me in subtle ways, and Dr Singh put pressure on in less subtle ways, for me to talk in Group, but I'd never heard her be so definite about it.

But the funny thing was, I sort of was ready to spill it. I nearly had to Oliver, outside, when we were having our smoke. If we'd been there any longer, I probably would have. I don't know what it was, maybe just that the time was right, maybe I trusted them now, maybe it was not having Cindy there any longer, but I did have this powerful desire to let it go. So I sat there hunched over hoping she wouldn't press me anymore, hoping she wouldn't ask any more questions, but also hoping she would.

There was such a long silence that I finally gave in and broke it. They do that a lot here, use silence to make people talk. It's pretty powerful, pretty effective. So at last I mumbled, "Everyone knows why I'm in here."

Marj said, "Perhaps you could tell us in your own words."

As I sat there thinking about that I made up my mind to say something about the whole mess with Rider Group. But when I did open my mouth I heard my voice say, to my big surprise: "I'm here because I killed my dog."

fourteen

CHECKERS WAS NOT the brightest dog there was, I've never claimed that for him. Actually he was pretty dumb in a lot of ways. Finding the rabbit at Clifford College, that was about the smartest thing he did. He did an awful lot of dumb things. He nearly gave me a heart attack one day when we were in the park and I suddenly realised he'd taken off and gone right across the street and was sniffing around the Mannings' place. Without thinking I called him and for once he spun around and came racing straight back. What I hadn't noticed was a car and trailer coming along the street, quite fast. Checkers saw the car: that wasn't the problem. The problem was, he didn't see that it was towing something. He swerved around the back of the car and looked like he was going to run full pelt into the trailer. At the very last second, though, he saw it and somehow managed to launch himself through the gap. Talk about timing. I wish I'd had a camera. Considering the speed of the car, I don't know how he did it, but I don't think a hair on his body was touched.

I suppose I was the dumb one really, calling him without making sure the road was clear.

But no, he was no genius, Checkers. What he had, and what I loved about him, was his happiness, his friendliness, his loyalty. He bounced through life, looking for another adventure, another game, another person to love and lick and fuss over. Those crazy black and white squares: you could see them a mile away, spreading chaos and confusion. It wasn't just Muggins, the Whites' cat, who suffered. Down the street were the Owenses, who had two borzois, dogs that looked like they belonged on the front cover of *Home and Garden.* They were perfectly groomed, perfectly beautiful, and perfectly boring. I never had Checkers on a leash in Argyle Street because it's such a quiet neighbourhood and every time we walked along it, Checkers would make a point of trotting across the road to the Owenses' house and barking through the high fence at their dogs. There'd be an immediate eruption inside as the two borzois barked their lungs out. Checkers, having stirred them up, would trot happily away again, a look of quiet satisfaction on his face. For five minutes or more, until we were a couple of blocks away, I'd hear the barking of the beautiful boring borzois. I thought Checkers and I were doing the dogs a big favour, giving them the only moment of excitement in their day, but the Owenses, who were as stupid and boring as their dogs, didn't agree. They complained to Dad, and I had to take a different route with Checkers.

I knew I felt bad about Checkers's death but I don't think I even knew myself how bad I felt until I said it in Group. And I didn't realise I felt guilty about it. Since Group, everyone keeps telling me that I shouldn't feel guilty—but it doesn't seem to help much. What you feel is what you feel.

When the snow holiday was over we went back to living in a fortress. And it really did become one. Dad had always refused to have a lot of security. "If they're going to get in, they're going to get in," he said. That's what he used to say. Now we had a remote control lock, intercom, video camera at the front and back gates, a new security fence all around the property and burglar alarms with flashing blue lights and loud sirens. A security company drove past about six times every night, and we had panic buttons to press that called them instantly if we ever needed them.

It was horrible. It made the house dark and horrible. I didn't look forward to coming home anymore and used to stay at school longer and longer in the afternoons.

For once Dad started to think getting Checkers might have been a good idea, because now Checkers could qualify as a guard dog. He probably became a tax deduction.

Checkers had gone berserk when we picked him up from the kennels. "He was very good," the lady said, "no trouble at all." But he'd lost weight. When we arrived to get him I saw him before he saw me. He was lying in his cage, on the strip at the front, with his nose almost under the gate and a little damp patch where he'd been breathing onto the concrete. I gave my special whistle that he always recognised, and his head shot up like he'd just touched a live wire with his tongue. He looked around wildly, his big eyes staring, trying to work out where the sound had come from. Then he saw me and he was on his feet whining and wagging his whole bottom, not just his tail. He kept pawing at the gate with his foot. When the woman started unlocking the gate, Checkers was down on his forepaws, still whining, like he couldn't, wouldn't, believe this was true until he was actually out. Then he got a glimpse of freedom. That was all it took. The woman had to sway out of the way as this mad collection of black and white leapt straight at my face. I ended up sitting on the concrete myself as Checkers climbed all over me, licking my face, making little crying noises, his welcome breath hot on my skin. It took about five minutes to get a lead on him. When I did, he dragged me to the car like I was a sled and he was a husky in a hurry to get to the South Pole.

My beautiful crazy ugly Checkers, so full of life, so much spirit and energy.

It was no wonder Dad wanted to turn the house into a fortress because the Vandals and Goths were at the drawbridge. It got quite scary. There were reporters and cameramen most days, sometimes one of each, sometimes two or three of each. A few weirdos turned up: a guy who explained over the intercom that he wanted to tell Dad how to dedicate his life to the One True Lord, another guy who said he had commercial information of enormous value to Dad and he would let him have it for $250,000, a woman who said she thought Dad was her real father whom she'd been searching for since 1986. Some of the other directors of Rider Group, Dermot and Doug, and a Mr Brooks, whom I didn't know too well, got into the habit of calling round late at night, and they and Dad would sit in his office for hours drinking and talking, with the door shut and no-one else allowed in. Jack never came round, not once, and we didn't go round there. I got the feeling that he and Dad weren't getting on so well now.

The next big story came with news that Jack had sold a large parcel of shares in Rider Group, which didn't exactly help the situation. I don't think Dad was too thrilled about that.

On November the eighth the *Standard* ran a story about the Premier's son. It said he was employed as a consultant by the American group who had advised Rider Group on their casino bid, and he'd been paid between three and four hundred thousand dollars. Everyone denied that and the Premier said he was taking legal action. Next day he and his son both issued writs against the *Standard.* On November the eleventh the *Argus* said Rider Group had illegally moved another twenty-eight million dollars offshore in September. November the fourteenth was a Sunday, but no rest for us. The *Sunday Spectator* had a big story that they advertised on TV all through the weekend. I think Dad and Jack tried to get an injunction to stop it, but they couldn't. The story was an interview with a bloke who'd worked as a gardener at the Premier's home, until he got the sack. He'd seen Dad on TV and he said he recognised him as a man who'd come to the Premier's house one day around the middle of March. "I noticed him because of the way he acted," he said. "It was like he was being smuggled into the place. Mr Koneckny brought him through a side gate. It was the only time I ever saw that gate used. They went across the back of the tennis court and into the house through the laundry door. They were looking around all the time, like they didn't want anyone to see them. They didn't see me, because I was in the greenhouse, but the bloke I saw that day was the same man I saw on TV."

On November the fifteenth the Premier stood up in Parliament and made a statement that the evening news showed in full, and that the papers ran the next day: "Once and for all I do not know Mr Murray Warner. He has never visited my house. I have never discussed the casino or the business affairs of Rider Group with him. The gardener referred to in yesterday's *Spectator* was dismissed from my employment for an unsatisfactory attitude to his work. If the *Standard* wishes to print these scurrilous stories from disaffected ex-employees they will have to face the legal consequences. I do not plan to spend the rest of the year answering these charges. This is my last word on the matter."

Then it was November the sixteenth. The day everything came to an end.

I'd been walking Checkers, as usual. I was feeling funny: lonely and depressed. The neighbours didn't seem to be talking to us the way they used to. My friends at school were getting kind of funny too, like wary, suspicious, and I sure wasn't making any new friends. Dad never seemed to talk to anyone at home, and he wasn't home much to talk to us anyway. Mum was weird: she'd taken to watching TV in an upstairs sitting room that no-one ever used. She sat there for hours every day with the lights off, just watching junk. She never used to watch TV before. When she wasn't doing that she was in her room, asleep. Mark was at his friends' practically full-time and when he was home he stayed in his room too. As a family we only came together at meals and the conversation was just grunts or sentences of two or three words.

The ski trip had worked for a while to improve things, but the effect didn't last long.

So there I was, wandering back along the street, being towed by Checkers, who was tired but wasn't going to admit it. We got to our place and I saw a reporter sitting on the bit of wall that they all seemed to choose. The stonework must have been nice and warm there. This guy was young, much younger than any others I'd seen. He looked about nineteen. He had long hair and this cool blue cap that was completely round and sat on his head like a cap on a bottle. He had a few pimples but they hardly showed. I admit I liked the looks of him but he wasn't taking any notice of me. He was looking at Checkers, staring at him, as though he was the greatest dog he'd ever seen. That attracted me to him too: I liked people who liked Checkers.

Above all, though, I think the reason I spoke to him was that I was so lonely.

He kept staring at Checkers as we walked towards him, but then he sort of pulled himself together and looked at me.

"Interesting dog," he said. "Very unusual looks."

I laughed. "That's one way of putting it."

"Well, I like him. He's got a nice honest face."

"Thanks."

"He's still a pup, isn't he?"

"Oh yes. Just a kid."

"How long have you had him?"

"Look," I said, because I'm not a complete fool and I'd dealt with these guys before, "if you want to talk to my father you're wasting your time. He won't be home for hours, and he probably won't talk to you when he does get here."

The guy looked quite hurt. "I know that," he said. "I wasn't trying to get around you. I really do like dogs."

Then I felt guilty—see, even then I suffered from that disease.

"Sorry," I said. "I'm just suspicious of all you guys now."

"I know," he said. "Some of them make me ashamed to be a journo. There's some real animals in this business." He looked at Checkers. "Sorry, mate," he said. "I didn't mean to insult animals."

"Which paper are you from?" I asked.

"The *Mail.* Not the *Standard.* We haven't given you too hard a time."

"You haven't given us a good time," I said.

He shrugged and looked away. "It's a complicated business."

I went to unlock the gate.

"Wait!" he said, jumping up and putting out his arm. He seemed so anxious to stop me. "We don't have to talk about Rider Group. It's boring sitting out here. Let's talk about something else. Your dog, if you want."

I admit I was flattered. And I suppose I thought if I got on well with this guy his paper might go easier on Dad.

"What's his name?" the man asked.

"Checkers."

He laughed, then stopped himself. "Sorry I laughed. It's a perfect name in every way, I think. When did you get him?"

"March."

"Oh yes? I've got a birthday in March. Which day'd you get him?"

"The sixteenth."

"Oh. My birthday's the twenty-third. So where'd you get him from?"

"Oh, some friend of Dad's. I don't know exactly."

"Was he a pup when you got him?"

"Yes."

"Has he got any brothers or sisters?"

"One, I think. What do you want to know so much about Checkers for?"

"I told you, I like dogs." He started to take his camera out of his bag. He didn't have a photographer with him.

"What are you doing?" I asked nervously. "No photos."

"You don't mind do you? It's not for the paper."

"What, you want to take a photo of Checkers for your own collection? Come off it."

"Not Checkers," he said. "You."

My face burned. "Don't be stupid."

"I'm not being stupid. You're stunning. I've got a lot of friends in advertising and modelling who'd kill to get a face like yours on their books. But, to be honest, I want to take it for myself. I don't want to forget you in a hurry."

I didn't know what to think. I was embarrassed, confused, but somewhere inside I was a bit pleased, I suppose thinking about how I could casually drop this into the conversation at school tomorrow. I took my time unlocking the gate and he fired off four or five shots.

"I've got to go," I said. "Come on, Checkers."

The guy looked at his camera. "Only got one or two left," he said. "Might as well use them up."

He pointed the camera at Checkers and, as I dragged him through the gate, he took a series of photos; more like ten than one or two. "Must have had more film left than I thought," he said.

I felt rude shutting the gate in his face, but I was still confused about him. So before I shut the gate I said, "My father normally gets home about eight o'clock. I'll ask him to talk to you if you want, but you've got to promise to be nice to him."

"It's OK," he said, like he didn't care anymore, which was another thing that confused me.

"You don't want to talk to him now?"

"No, I've got to get back to the office. Anyway eigh o'clock's too late for me." He was backing away toward his car, then with a quick wave he went around to th driver's door. Seemed like suddenly he was in a bi hurry. I shrugged and closed the gate. I'd been attracted to him at first but now I was starting to think he was a bit strange. And I didn't like the idea of his having photos of me.

fifteen

DAD LEFT FOR WORK about seven the next morning, which was late for him. But it seemed like almost no time before I heard his car again, in the driveway. There was a furious spitting of gravel and a squeal of tyres. The sounds, so angry and alien, frightened me. I jumped out of bed and ran to the front door and opened it. Dad was already on the veranda and coming straight at the door. If I hadn't opened it I think he'd have gone through it. His face: I'd never seen him looking like that. It was black, dark with rage, shadowed. His lips were trembling. "Get out of my way," he said. He didn't look at me. I could have been a shop dummy. He pushed me aside, violently. I fell backwards over the umbrella stand, against the wall. "What?" I said. He was already down the hallway and going into the kitchen. I stood up again and put the umbrella stand upright, then followed him, nervously. When I came into the kitchen he had one of the cutlery drawers open and was fumbling through it

He pulled out a long sharp carving knife. “What are you doing?” I asked him. He didn’t answer.

I’d got up earlier to let Checkers out and I could hear him now, whining at the back door. Dad went to the door and threw it open. He put his knee into Checkers, really brutally, to keep him out. “Don’t,” I called, but I was too scared to go after him. He went outside, with Checkers. I couldn’t see what was happening. At that moment the phone rang. I picked up the kitchen one without even moving: it was right at my elbow. I heard Jack’s voice asking, “Who’s that?” I told him. “You,” he said. “You’ve done it for us now, you stupid bitch. You and your stupid father.”

“What do you mean?” I asked, in a frightened whisper.

“Have a look at the paper,” he said. The line went dead. I remembered that Dad had dropped a newspaper as he was coming across the veranda. It was probably all over the front garden by now. I ran to get it. On the way I bumped into Mum.

“What’s going on?” she asked. “Why’s he back?”

“I don’t know.” They’re the last words I’ve spoken to her. I came out onto the veranda. I was right about the paper: it was everywhere, so many sheets blowing around the lawn that it looked like a snowstorm. I grabbed at one: it was a page of classified ads.

I let it go and ran around looking for the news section. From the back of the house came a terrible high-pitched squeal, a shriek that seemed to tear through my body. I felt like a dark cloud had come over the sky, over the house. I was in a state of terror, hysteria, I suppose.

I grabbed at another sheet that blew past me and there it was: two photos of Checkers and a screaming headline. I stared at the huge black print, trying to read the words. Eventually I made sense of them: EXPLAIN THIS, MR PREMIER. Explain what? What did Checkers have to do with the Premier? I stared frantically at the page, wanting to work it out but wanting to rush out to the back garden too, to see what terrible thing had happened, what had caused Checkers to utter that ghastly wail. I scanned the article, trying to take it in quickly, even as I was moving back to the front door, down the corridor.

"The long reign of Bruce Scranton seems certain to come to an end late this morning. The Premier will face the party room at 11 A.M., and is expected to be presented with an ultimatum: resign or be sacked. And the cause of his downfall? A young black and white dog named Checkers. A dog that belongs to a man the Premier says he has never met." That was the opening. Then came another, smaller headline: DOG THE MISSING LINK IN CASINO INVESTIGATION. Under that the article began: "Months of rumour and innuendo about the Premier's involvement with Rider Group came to a head last night when the teenage daughter of a Rider Group executive admitted to the *Mail* that the family's pet dog was a personal gift from the Premier. The dog was handed over at a secret meeting between the Premier and Rider Group's Finance Director, Murray Warner. The man the Premier still claims he has never met!" Now was shaking uncontrollably. JUDGE FOR YOURSELF, read the next heading. "The Premier's dog and his brother! Can you tell them apart?" Only then did I realise that the two photos I'd thought were of Checkers were of two dogs: Checkers and another one. They could have been twins: in fact, they were. "Faced with an unwanted puppy, from a litter of two, in March of this year the Premier did what most of us do: gave one away to someone who owed him a favour. Someone who owed him a billion-dollar favour! Someone whom Premier Scranton has consistently claimed, both inside and outside Parliament, he has never met."

At the bottom of the page were all the previews of the stories on inside pages: BRUCE SCRANTON: SURVIVED FOURTEEN YEARS OF INQUIRIES AND ROYAL COMMISSIONS — BROUGHT DOWN BY A DOG: PAGE 2; MUTTON OR FULLATON TIPPED FOR TOP JOB: PAGE 3; WHAT WILL HAPPEN TO CASINO CONTRACT?: PAGE 4; THE WESTMINSTER TRADITION: MINISTERS WHO MISLEAD PARLIAMENT: PAGE 5; ANOTHER FAMOUS DOG NAMED CHECKERS: PRESIDENT RICHARD NIXON: PAGE 6; EDITORIAL: ONE SCANDAL TOO MANY: PAGE 22.

I let the paper go, although later I was to get it back and read it compulsively, to make myself sick, like an itch that you scratch and scratch even though you know you'll make it red and hot and sore. I never bothered denying all the lies in it. Come to think of it, no-one ever asked me whether I'd actually said all those things. I guess they just took it for granted that I had.

I walked through the house to the kitchen. Dad was sitting at the kitchen table with his head in his hands. I walked past him and out through the door to the lawn.

Checkers was lying there in a pool of blood. His face was contorted in its last spasm of agony and fear and confusion. I sat there in the blood and cradled him, rocking him to sleep.

sixteen

I DON'T KNOW if talking in Group helped. Once I started, I couldn't stop. That was funny; I hadn't expected that. I talked for about a week. Well, it seemed like that to me. I know it wasn't quite that way, but it seemed . . .

Oh well. It doesn't matter.

That was more than three weeks ago. Since then I suppose I've been a bit better. They seem to think so here, Marj and Dr Singh and Sister Llosa. They've put me on the Patients' Committee for instance. I get to welcome new patients, collect suggestions to improve the place, listen to complaints about the food, stuff like that.

There sure have been plenty of new patients to welcome. I'm the only one left of our little group. Ben went home. I don't think he was much better, or that he'd learnt much, but he went home anyway. Esther went to live with her grandmother, the one she doesn't like, and her father. Her mother said she wanted some time to herself, so Esther couldn't go to her. Emine went home.

She was really nervous about it but it was her decision: she didn't want to stay here any longer.

Daniel went home three days ago. He was good: his showers were down to ten minutes, which makes them shorter than mine. Maybe he passed his disease on to me. Oliver went home today. That was awful. I've been dreading it for more than a week. I didn't cry in front of him but God I bawled my eyes out after he'd gone. I don't love him or anything like that: it's just that he became my best friend, so close to me that I could tell him anything.

He gave me his phone number and all that stuff. I'll ring him tomorrow. I hope we can talk. The nurses say that friendships formed in here don't usually survive outside. I hope they're wrong.

I miss them all, Ben and Cindy and Oliver and Emine and Esther and Daniel, I miss them all. They became my brothers and sisters.

And now I go around the place welcoming their replacements.

They're not too easy to welcome, though. They're so nervous, so messed up when they come in here. I go into their rooms to introduce myself and tell them how the place works and most of them look at me like I'm an axe murderer or serial killer, like, if they make a false move I'll attack them with my ballpoint pen. I don't blame them. I was that way, too. Being in a psych hospital, God, I just knew they were going to put me in a padded cell or a straitjacket and leave me here for twenty years.

For example, I've learned not to stand between new patients and the doors of their rooms—even that makes them nervous.

The most common question here has always been "what are you in for?" but I never ask it too soon. I figure you've got to get to know people a bit first. Not like Daniel: he loved asking. He couldn't wait to find out. Half the time he just got stupid answers, though. Cindy used to say she was allergic to pumpkin.

Some people say they've got the "s" word: that's schizophrenia. Some people say they've got the "a" word: that's anorexia. Some people just say "Depression." Some people just show you the scars on their wrists.

But gradually, no matter what they say, you figure it out. So now we have Beth, who's got bulimia. There's Tony, who's in a wheelchair, but he's meant to be really violent. There's Jacqui, who's been expelled from four schools and run away from home a hundred times. There's Nick, who gets panic attacks and can't breathe. There's Tanya, who cuts herself, not like slashing her wrists, but just, I don't know, because she wants to I suppose. And there's a new girl, I don't know her name or what she's here for. I guess she's replacing Oliver. She came in a couple of hours ago. Tomorrow I'll have to go and do my welcoming routine: "Good morning and welcome to the funny farm. We hope you enjoy your stay. This resort has everything you could ever ask for, including Mr Miles who'll try to take you into the Men's so he can grope you and Max who thinks the CIA are after him and Bernadette who'll wake you up in the middle of the night trying to strangle you. Don't worry, though, she's not strong enough to do it. Have a nice day."

I think if I had anywhere to go they'd probably discharge me pretty soon, too. But with Dad not getting bail and Mum still not capable of looking after herself, let alone anyone else, they're not quite sure what to do with me. I'll probably do like Mark and go to boarding school. I don't know about the holidays. I think Mark's going to stay with friends from Clifford College. Probably Josh. Mark's lucky; he's still got friends from his old school. I don't think I do. It's two months since I heard from anyone from my school.

Maybe I'll just stay here forever, welcoming people and saying goodbye to people. I might be the first permanent member of the Patients' Committee. Safe in here, safe and secure, protected from the piranhas, not having to think about my family and my friends and how I killed my darling dog, Checkers.